Anonymous

Athelstan

A Poem

Anonymous

Athelstan
A Poem

ISBN/EAN: 9783337398033

Printed in Europe, USA, Canada, Australia, Japan

Cover: Foto ©Andreas Hilbeck / pixelio.de

More available books at **www.hansebooks.com**

ATHELSTAN:

A POEM.

————— —

LONDON:

EDWARD MOXON & CO., DOVER STREET.

1862.

BOOK I.

Noise choked the narrow streets of Winchester,
A noise to rouse the morning from its bed,
When steel met steel, and heart encounter'd heart
With the keen hate of hours.   The sombre air
Was tortured into sound, as arrows whirr'd
Like birds of iron beak, and missive spears
Knock'd at the breasts that fronted them, to seek
An entry into life—alas ! for man
That such a scene where ghastly wounds unmake
The beauty which God made of face and form
Should have a grandeur in it !   'Tis the stake,
The chance of loss in such a mortal game,
That turns red carnage from a murd'rous fiend
To a destroying angel.   On one side,

The smaller number'd, there were ranged a few
With better arms, and bearing more composed,
For the stern work they handled : at their head
Was Ælfred, the ambitious Ætheling.
He, fighting for a crown, of such an aim
Fought worthy, throwing into voice and arm
The weight of his great venture ; with each shout
That cheer'd his friends, he struck a foe to earth.*

The fight was straiten'd by the little breadth
Of the old city's threads of winding road,
Where buildings of all sorts, some timber-ribb'd,
Tall, and stone-corner'd, others shed-like, thatch'd
With broad-leaf'd water-flags, stood opposite
With slender interval ; where fortress-house

* Historically the opposition of Ælfred to Athelstan's succession, is surrounded with numerous difficulties. On what he founded his claims to succeed the son of the Great Alfred, has never been explained, and is, perhaps, not susceptible of explanation ; but that foul play was used toward him cannot be doubted. Rome has always been ready to oblige such princes as have displayed an inclination to enrich its treasury, which Athelstan's policy, as well as his superstition, induced him to do ; and therefore we are little surprised at the series of tragical incidents which terminated Ælfred's career.

Of noble Thane, jostled the shiv'ring hut

That crouch'd beside it ; or the huckster's shop,

With all its small display of daily wares

Spread out and open to the air and eye,

Fronted a palace of the priests of Christ.

Adown the central lane a wavy crowd

Of men pour'd, struggling in uncertain fray,

On dashing, or forced backward as the luck

Of victory bore them—'twas the profitless rage

Of party-passion, and the taste of blood

That turn'd the current of humanity :

Men slew their neighbours, and then scream'd for joy.

Half-arm'd, and arm'd, and unarm'd citizens,

And old and young, struck out, and stabb'd, or tore

With naked hands, dyeing their clothes with blood

As the true colour of their loyalty.

Amid the many combatants were two

Pre-eminent in noise and action ; one

Was young and tall, and angularly built,

And strong, and quick of limb, nor over-clothed.

His features had a false and wasted look,

The ineffaceable stamp of suffering vice.

The other was a portlier man, though short,

And drest in such habiliments as mark'd

A lot which Fortune had made comfortable.

His syrce was wove of linen ; to his knee

Adorn'd with trimmings, loosely flow'd and large

His linen tunic, while his feet were housed

Within an old similitude of shoes :

But, to leave free his movements, he had left

His decent sagum safely hung at home.

'Twas a strong party-feeling which had forced

The citizen to risk his gotten wealth

And the few years of life which yet remain'd

To make him own himself an aged man.

The two fought boldly on opposing sides,

And 'mid the thick confusion of the fray

The younger sought the elder, for he strove

With earnestness as deep as was the taste
He nurtured for the baser joys of earth,
To take the life of the old citizen,
And by one stroke to cancel for all time
The moneys that he owed him :—what the use
Of paying those with sublunary coin
Whose dead hands close not on it, when 'tis given ?

At last they met—one desperately brave,
And staking all he lived for on a blow ;
The other timid, lest from the same hole
Whence life escaped, he might let slip the chance
Of seeing his lent gold come home again.
In the short fight, the elder combatant
Let pass some chances, for the miser's soul
Restrain'd the arm, from doing all its ill,
And strove to overpower the youth, but not
Disable him from payment.   A strong blow
Which broke his guard, and beat him down to earth,
Show'd how his wisdom was pure foolishness.

There lay he in his imbecility,

And swore to spare the payment of the debt

In payment for his life.   The victor smiled

A most unchristian smile, and cried, " My friend !

One fact is worth ten possibilities.

The living may keep promises ; the dead

Can never break them.   Thou'rt my prize by right

Of lawful war,—thus I dispose of thee."

And with a thud he dropt his heavy maul

Upon the wrinkled front.   The old man's eyes

Closed in eternal night, and his last thoughts

Mix'd horribly up the matters of two worlds,

God's coming judgment, and his stolen gold.

But now one party—'twas the weaker one,

Which its rash venture without standing-place

'Twixt death and victory, had made doubly bold—

Was press'd on by the opposite partisans,

O'erweighted backwards ; on its flank there rush'd

From a side alley an impetuous crowd

Of fighters, fresh and shrieking for the fray.

Forced on two points, the others were swept down

The narrow and uneven street, that show'd

No outlet at the ending, and there stood,

Some lacking room to strike, while others fell

Down-trodden, lying without sense or sound.

An ancient cross, hewn hastily of stone,

Arose close by, and up its rounded steps

Their leader, Ælfred, sprang, and stretch'd his arms

Motioning silence,—'twas a novelty

That pleased the crowd an instant—then he cried,

" What have I done, my countrymen ? The wish

To rule brave men like you, is that a crime

To die for ? Born of royal parentage,

And of true man and wife, is that a fault

To blush for ? Honest Saxons ! would ye have

A bastard for your king ? Choose Athelstan !

Where is prince Ethelwald ?*—suspiciously

* It will be immediately perceived, that in my theory of Athelstan's
character, I agree with Mr. St. John, who, in his " History of the

He slipt from life ; and do ye love a man

Who slew his brother ?—then take Athelstan ——"

More had he said, but a thick grim-faced man,

Half naked, and with ugly unshaved skin,

Uglier with blood, seized a large log, and hurling

Hit Ælfred on the brow ; the fickle crowd

Broke into laugh and action all at once,

And pierced right through the band of followers, mass'd

Between them and the speaker : him they clutch'd,

And bore off captive with such lusty shouts

As would beseem a victory o'er the Dane.

His friends then, indiscriminately mix'd

With the opponent rabble, wisely hid

four Conquests of England," has given a totally new interpretation of this period of our annals. The bastard son of Edward the Elder, succeeding to the throne by ability, not by right, maintained his position, and delivered himself from all the chances of rivalry which he dreaded, by means the most unscrupulous. There is no actual proof that he made away with the eldest of his legitimate brothers, though the opportune rapidity with which he disappeared from the scene, coupled with several instances in Athelstan's life, seems to justify the worst suspicions. The passage in Mr. St. John's history is as follows :—"The brother next to him in years, and born in wedlock, might perhaps have disputed his title; but a sudden and mysterious death overtook him at Oxford, and a few days saw him laid in the royal tomb beside his father." Vol. i. p. 332.

All opposition and its signs, and saved
Worse present consequence, till time supplied
Sure means of safety in a homeward flight.

So the crowd dragg'd away their prisoner,
Crying, " Down Ælfred ! up with Athelstan !"
But Athelstan, though eloquent of tongue,
Was not found there to speak ; and Athelstan,
Although the very bravest call'd him brave,
Was not found there to strike the blow he could.
And the mass, gathering numbers as they roll'd,
Conveying Ælfred with rude hands to front
The royal presence, shouted " Athelstan ! "
With growing zeal,—and was it not enough
That thus the unsolicited populace
He sought for subjects should eject his name
From their free throats in clamorous praise to Heav'n ?

Vain was the royal blood in Ælfred's veins ;
Vain his descendance from a wedded love.

The bar he held across the onward path
Of Athelstan to pow'r, was snapt in twain
As the plant-stems on India's woody hills
Are broken when the wild bull, square in form
Of bulky grandeur, meets them in his path
Resistless, frighten'd by the hunter's fire.
But if the wise king press'd with heavy hand
Upon the foil'd rebellious Ætheling,
How could he shield off the keen arrows shot
From blaming lips, inspired by hearts that hate?

Where could both-sided justice, firm in power,
And strong of eye to see the shades of wrong
From crime to flaw, and fit them with a scourge,
Be found in Europe if not found in Rome?
There dwelt Heaven's friends—a light thing deem'd
      they it,
That by a chance their judgment should be judged
By much-mistaken mortals uninspired.

How, then, dispose of this rebellious Prince?

Send him to Rome!—and so to Rome he went.

And when men go to Rome unwillingly,

Not always can they quit it when they will.

Yet whence arose the tale which Ælfred told

About the graceless birth of Athelstan?

Fair was Edwina,* she who caught the eye

Of royal Edward; 'twas a simple life

The maiden led as guardian of her sheep,

Yet could not guard her heart, which Love, more fierce

Than the fear'd wolf, had ravish'd from her breast,

Nor ask'd the church to register the wrong.

She dreamt a dream one night of summer-time,

---

* The circumstances of Athelstan's birth, which few historians have been at the pains to investigate, are full of the elements of romance, and hardly therefore need any embellishment from fiction. They already lie within the domains of poetry, and it is only necessary to expand the statements of the Chroniclers to render them fit to match with the wildest inventions. Athelstan, by the splendour, if not by the virtues of his reign, reflected lustre on his Shepherd Mother.

That she gave birth to a full-circled moon,
Which, raised aloft, lit England's general land,
Shining on lordly turret, the round arch
Of cold cathedral, and on wattled hut.
So, when the time was come, Edwina bore
Into the living and substantial world
The light of England, Athelstan the Great.

But how the pair,—one regal by his birth,
The other by her beauty,—roam'd the woods,
And found the rough roads level to their feet,
Nor felt the rain-drops pattering on their heads,
Nor heeded clammy dews, nor headlong sun,
And suffer'd sheep to stray unwittingly,
And let men more unruly rule themselves,
It matters not to tell.   Time too will bring
The weight of years to crush e'en Love to death ;
And so they past away, and left behind
The memory of an unwise preference,
Which virtue chides, and weakness imitates.

Wide stretch'd o'er many an acre of rich ground

Stood an old abbey, that of Malmesbury.*

Wall'd in with arches semicircular,

And intersecting each its neighbouring curve,

It open'd its main entries ; northward one,

And one to the warm south.   In rude detail

Of inartistic ornament it rose,

Square-mass'd, and shelter'd by quick-sloping roofs.

But its small windows, parted each from each

By balusters of clumsy-statured stone,

Lack'd not for paintings, strongly imaging

---

* Whoever is familiar with the "Monasticon," will be aware that in describing Malmesbury Abbey, I have by no means exaggerated the gloomy grandeur impressed by our ancestors on the favorite dwelling-places of the monks. Scattered all over England, in the most beautiful of its beautiful woods and valleys, they displayed, from the commencement, all the pomp of the architectural genius possessed by inventive barbarism, which dealt with stone as if it had been clay, and fashioned it into a thousand fantastic shapes, to excite surprise, and dazzle the imagination. Until after the middle of the seventh century the abbey of Malmesbury continued poor, and insignificant; it was then brought into notice by the genius of a Scotch monk, and soon afterwards received an augmentation of fame by the poetry and preaching of Aldhelm. The man, however, who really rendered it historical, was the florid and flattering monk, William, who, in spite of his faults, has contributed a mass of useful materials to English History.

The works of saints, and stranger miracles
Than their first Master, in the exercise
Of His great sympathy, divinely wrought.

'

Nor wanted there, as elsewhere, the chill sense
Of an unearthly presence, felt by men—
Material things of limitable days—
In the dread temples of the unseen God,
Around whose precincts, and within whose walls
The formless dead, we fancy, crowd the spots
Where lie their bodies, lifting bony hands
To Heav'n, in fearful and perpetual pray'r;
While through the aisles past ages seem to roll
In cloudy sequence, from whose depths a voice
Murmurs, "Tho' ancient, we are naught when stretch'd
Against the measure of eternity."

So rose it, strong and beautiful in stone,
And arch'd and aisled and flank'd and intercross'd,
And many-chamber'd inwardly, being made

For uses of a comfortable faith,

That fills the body to sustain the soul.

It was much blest with relics, also blest

With the earth's perishable wealth, the dross

Which answers all things, and is sought by all.

There came the man of mind, who deem'd the world

Too wicked, and himself too good for work,

And found a shelter in those holy aisles,

From his contaminating brotherhood.

There came the man of action, who had sinn'd

Until the wish, if not the means, for more

Had vanish'd with the practice.   For example,

Take the old Thane, the high-born Sigeric,

Well cut and polish'd to the social scale

Which the world uses in conferring rank,

And measuring out admissibilities.

He sinn'd no more than the indulgent times,

Coarse in themselves, and human hearts at large,

Still coarser in their passions, thought was fair.

Rich was he, and being noble too, was deem'd

                                                   C

To have no balance for mere charity,

And such things, when the year's expenditure

Had satisfied the exigence of rank,

And the stern claims which self had made on self;

For Pleasure ask'd large outlay for her needs,

And was allow'd it; yet he was not bold

In vicious life, for his timidity

Of nature forced him try to outstrip thought

When in pursuit of some luxurious sin.

And so when old, and satiate in taste,

And worn in purse, his feeble spirit took

Another turn—another phase of fear,

Of possibilities of untried worlds,

And troublesome examination-days,

With conscience to give evidence in court,

Perplex'd him, then within the abbey walls

He shut his body, and contrived to hope

He shut all further consequence without.

What could he better do than thus to spend

The balance of his wealth and life,—the one

He gave the monks to use for Heaven and him ;

The other he wore out in harmless sleep,

And days of penitential idleness.

On a hard seat of carven wood that graced

The abbey's inmost chamber, sat a man

Of middle height and years, for action framed,

And in whose form was strongly prominent

The power to serve the soul, that on his brow

Like a king throned, thought quickly, and then gave

Its edicts forth for action, crying " Do ! "

And it was done.   His sire and mother both

Had past their beauty down to him ; but still

There dwelt upon his gracious lineaments

A something all his own, an anxious look

Such as the brave might wear, who fear, though brave,

Being sensitive, lest they be thought to fear :

His cloak, of double silk, and with an edge

Of precious ermine deep, was drawn with art

Across both shoulders, while in front a brooch—

A dazzling diamond, set in golden rays

Alternating with ebony, like sun

With shade—confined it to his manly breast.

Down to his bosom, ringleted in gold

And interlacen much with golden thread,

Flow'd the long twists of his luxuriant hair.

Such was the princely man who sat and spake

To the meek abbot standing by his side,

Meek as a listener should be when the speaker

Was the crown'd king of Wessex' broad demesnes,

The light of England, Athelstan the Great.*

Then said the king, " Sir Abbot, it was fit

That the loud people's throat should consecrate

---

* In person, Athelstan was of middle height; his countenance displayed the hereditary beauty of his family, and was shaded by that luxuriant golden hair for which the Anglo-Saxons were so long remarkable; and, to augment its splendour, he habitually wore it intertwisted with threads of gold. (" History of the Four Conquests of England," vol. i. p. 351.) Nothing can exceed the meagreness of the Chroniclers when they speak of costume or personal ornaments; so that when we desire to form an accurate idea of our ancestors in those respects, we are compelled with the antiquarians to descend into their graves, where, as a provision apparently for the future, they habitually deposited whatever they regarded as most precious.

Our name with clamour, that the Church should bless

Our title to the throne, and smooth the seat

Which, at the best, jolts every sitter there,

Suggesting rubs and falls." Now he, the abbot,

Was a man blest with that good substitute

For better things called tact, which can so hide

Its ignorance behind a veil of hints,

And decent silence, and sly-featured looks,

To seem like knowledge in disguise, prepared

To throw its mask off when it wants to shine :

Yet, when the path was clear, he could advance

With rounded tongue in unimpeded talk

To please the listener when he sought to please,

And knew the method. "Who that heard," he cried,

" The voices raised at Kingston, when the crown

Was fix'd on brows which Nature built for it ;

(After the due and solemn obsequies

Of thy great sire performed at Winchester ;)

Who that there saw the bonfires shooting forth

Their myriad tongues, and piled by myriad hands,

Could doubt the general suffrage?   Some there were

Who zealous for a grander light to grace

The joyful day, rush'd to the hated house

Of Ælfred the rebellious Ætheling,

And wrenching all the wood-work from its place,

Rafter and door, and pillar'd bannister,

Heap'd up the hasty monument, and thrust

The reedy thatch in intervals betwixt ;

And when 'twas kindled, how the giant flame

Crush'd the poor timber in its fiery arms,

As if to extirpate avengingly

The last remains of treason : had e'en he

Thy brother Ethelward been present—"   " Nay ! "

Return'd the king, as on his earnest look

The shadow deepen'd, " Talk not now of him ;

Too recently hath fallen the sudden death

Of one so dear, who would have worn the crown

More worthily than we.   But now our grief

Lies buried with our brother Ethelward.

Let the two die if one cannot revive."

Then said the abbot, "'Tis your Grace's will"

(Meaning the will of monarchs must be right) ;

"But who so blinded by ambitious hate,

As not to see your Grace could ne'er have reach'd

So great a height, unlifted by God's arm ?

At Kingston—that old town of kings, fit place

For turning men to monarchs—with one heart

Stood forth the mitred princes of the land

Signalling Heav'n, and in their wishes call'd

Its lightnings down, to consecrate thy rule

And fall on heads of traitors."   "But they fell not,"

Cried Athelstan.   "Not so, my liege ! " replied

The abbot.   "Heav'n hath other messengers

Than visible flame, to blast its sinners with.

It sends a slow disease to sap the strength,

Or checks the play of some organic pulse

Whereby hangs life.   Reflect, my gracious lord,

On Ælfred's fate.   When prison'd by the people

After some little brush of opposition,

Convey'd to Rome, he pleaded for himself.—

But he were more than man who could impose

Upon that conclave of celestial wit—

What were his arguments, what matters it ?

For when he claim'd to swear his innocence

Upon St. Peter's altar, his voice broke,

Cut into stammers, and his eyes look'd mad,

As if some pain were pushing at their roots.

Then the high pontiff (in whose Heav'n-purged sight,

Your Grace, as the legitimate heir of Virtue,

And eldest-born of Wisdom, rules by right

More strong than chance-birth gives to knaves and

     fools)

Threw at the wretched noble such a look

As hath a venom in it for the bad,

But leaves the good unscathed ; and through his veins

There coursed a flood of fire retributive,

And shrieking, on the marble floor he fell,

Confusing prayers with curses, shifting back

From guilt professed to clamorous innocence

As the pains lessen'd.   Carried thence away

To his own home, he pined exceedingly,
And on the third day died.   Thus God removes
The mortal checks that do oppose His will—
And His will is to humble every foe
Before the footstool of King Athelstan !"

Half-pleased the king was, yet half-wearily
He listen'd, wiser than his age, but still
Not unimpress'd with small belief that Heav'n
Had lent the keys of Wisdom to a tribe ;
And joy it doubtless was to think his path
Was clearer by one foe, whate'er the means.
Then said he, " Now that we advance in arms
Against Northumbria, our insulted Church
Should let its blessings back the soldier's hope
Conclusive of success.   Thou knowest how Sihtric,
That fierce unmannerly Dane to whom we gave
Our sister and our holy faith at Tamworth
In marriage to the two, hath burst the bonds
That bound him both to Christ and Eadgitha.

Again the hog hath sought his sensual sty,

And wallows in the mire of paganism."

For true it was that Sihtric (who had donn'd

The pure white habit of a neophyte

To dress his new-born faith in) had embraced

A creed as lightly as he took a wife— *

For a convenient season,—till his taste

Or worldly interest prompted him to try

A fairer partner or a kinder god.

So when his evil thoughts resolved to change

Good things for chance of better, he bade lead

King Edward's daughter in barbaric pomp

Of noble and of priestly company,

---

* The relations of Sihtric with Athelstan are full of strange
interest, chiefly because they gave rise to that war, and series of
wild adventures which history is now only beginning to relate, and
which charmed me into the choice of the subject of my present poem.
Fratricides, marriages, sudden deaths, the overthrow of princes from
their thrones, the descent of princesses from the palace to the cloister,
the freaks of piracy, the wild gatherings of the north, the measuring
of the strength of England against that of half-a-dozen states
combined,—all these things arose out of one act of Sihtric, though
he disappears from the scene before even the immediate consequences
of his deeds: the remoter may affect us still.

Where Odin's temple stood, scoop'd half from earth,

And half piled up of rugged blocks of stone,

Like fragments nipp'd by giants from the rocks

To serve their warfare. Dark the cave-room spread

Its damp extent and vast, till placed around,

A thousand torches, like dumb voices, woke

Its silence into light. Then one might see

Where, on a marble pillar, helmeted,

The idol stood, the Pagan saint of war.

When Sihtric raised his right hand as to speak,

Suddenly every torch went out, as if

It closed its eyes upon the deeds to come.

But the fierce monarch, with his arm'd heel smiting

The hard soil, raised his loud incensèd voice,

Foreswore his double covenant, and cursed

The blameless Son of God : whereon a shudder

Ran over all things through th' invisible night ;

And the tall statue, breast-plate, shield, and banner

Shaking, men shriek'd lest it should fall on them,

And, by the seeing of fresh-kindled lights,

His casque appear'd so cloven, as in battle
Would have kill'd any warrior wearing it.

But the rough Dane held on to his intent,
And Eadgitha went back to Athelstan.
Simple she was in manners, with a heart
Not bold in right, but indolently kind,
She fenced herself within a little ring
Of pious forms and unoffending acts,
And, as she did no harm and wish'd no ill,
Seem'd comfortably credulous of Heav'n.

So when the king demanded from the Church
Its help to curse before he kill'd his foe,
"Sire," cried the abbot, "had your pious love
Not dower'd the church so richly with earth's goods,
(Among the rest the forfeit property
Of Ælfred, the rebellious Ætheling),
That, raised above the gross necessity
Of thinking for the morrow, she can give

To souls of men all dues of loving care,

In such a war, begun for Heav'n, her prayers

Would fill your banners with victorious breath ;

But now—"   Here entering spake a monk, and said,

" A lady come from York, the capital

Of Deira and Bernicia, where the Dane

Hath sinn'd the double sin 'gainst God and man,

Handmaiden to the princess Eadgitha,

Craves leave to utter what she hath to tell."

Admitted then spake Bertha, reverence made

Unto the king and his good counsellor,

" Sihtric, the royal fratricide, is dead ! "

Here her speech stopp'd, in too impetuous flow

Through the full channel of her utterance ;

And the king, rising quickly, look'd as one

That struggles with a foe whom in his soul,

He knows to be far mightier than himself,

Yet will not, in his pride of nature, show

The sense of a subordinate quality.

"Ay," went on Bertha, hastily, "the man

Who stept upon his elder brother's corpse

To mount a throne, hath been erased, they say,

By Heav'n's own finger, as a blot on Nature."

Then the king seem'd like him who hath obtain'd

A mastery o'er himself, and set his nerve

To rigid hardihood of suffering;

And slowly back his spirit came to him,

And swell'd his chest, and lit his light-blue eye

With the pleased sense of thinking how the death

Of the apostate Dane had smooth'd the path

'Twixt Wessex and the doom'd Northumbria.

Then, crying "Tell thy tale out," Bertha spake.

"Seven times the seventh night from that wherein

The Danish king forsook his covenant

With God and with your Grace, low in the heav'ns,

Where the North joins the East, uprose a cloud,

Leaving blue-bright the sky 'twixt it and earth.

Bow-like in shape, slowly its dark form grew

Instinct with light, when from its upper edge

Shot jets of flame, which, to the startled air,

Like to a fiery liquor spurted up.

From its cleft breast then brilliant pillars sprang,

Wid'ning and changing colours as they rose

From dazzling white to the deep hue of blood,

Till their high tops saluting the mid heav'n

Spread like an arch of fire.   Men gazed and shook

Beneath their idle armour, as through air

There rush'd a sound like that of hissing tongues

Chasing each other.   That same night the king

Was missing from the banquet—when at length

They forced his chamber-door, they found him curl'd

Upon the bed, with large round eyes, and arm

Stretch'd with the right palm outward, as in fear

Of something which he strove to keep from him.

Sihtric was dead !—So die all enemies

Of God and of the king !"   Then Athelstan :

" Who hath succeeded to this stricken prince

To bar the tide of our invading host,

Lest it o'erflow the land, and York be join'd

In stricter bond to London, than the tie

Which bound the Dane unto our sister's bed?"

"Anlaf and Guthforth," she rejoin'd, "the sons

Of the dead king, but chiefly Anlaf grasps

The reins of rule, as doth a charioteer

Who o'er the course with prudent courage guides

The hasty chariot."   Then her quick tongue ran

Over the young Dane's princely qualities,

As a fair field, where no unfriendly doubt

Check'd her expatiating; without a fault

She found him, but the fault, perchance, of virtue,

Which, with excess of impulse to one end,

Heeds not the things that in a crowded world

Should slacken action, and o'erturning wrong,

O'erturns the right too in its midway rush.

Then Athelstan, half-wond'ring, look'd at her,

And said, "So good, and yet an enemy

Of England and its king!"   And Bertha blush'd.

" A Pagan !" cried the priest, and Bertha sigh'd.

And the king said again, " Thou didst not leave

With thy good mistress when she left.   Great grace

It was that thou shouldst linger at thy choice,

And, when thou wouldst, couldst go by sufferance !"

He sought no answer, and she answer'd not.

" Lo !" cried the abbot, " Said I not that Heav'n

Strikes down the enemies of Athelstan ?

Advance, my lord, and grasp the good its hand

Miraculously tenders."   And the abbot

Added in thought, and thoughts occasionally

Prelude the wish, and this in active men

Runs into action ; but inertly shrewd

The abbot was, and so he merely thought

"The king will take Northumbria, of its spoils

A part may find its way to Malmesbury."

Then rose aloud throughout the general land

The cry, " To arms ! to arms !"   In Winchester

It burst, and onward roll'd to London town,

And London hurl'd it back to Winchester.

From village-huts the summons gather'd up

The soldier-peasants ; slightly clad they came :

Close-coated to the knee, a short cloak hung

O'er the left shoulder, buckled on the right

With clasps whose ornament bespoke their means.

For dull white linen most did substitute

The brown defence of leather ; heavy-limb'd,

Light-hair'd, light-eyed, they flock'd ; and some there

      were

Averse to turn away compelledly

To war from the safe industry of fields,

And from the unwash'd beauties of young wives.

But when they heard the din of driven nails

Upon rude breast-guards, and the shiv'ring twang

Of tested bow-strings, and beheld the gleam

Of pointed pikes, and held them in their hands,

They suck'd the common atmosphere around,

And from each other's presence, and the shouts

Of brawny throats, and stories of won fights,

Catching the bloody sympathy of war
Like fever in their veins, they thought no more
Of home, and the small children training up
To take their places if themselves were slain.

   A knot of talkers sat or stood or lay
Round a huge fire one night of early spring.
'Twas in a hall—or call it otherwise—
A room low-roof'd, small-window'd, and thick-wall'd.
The men who fill'd it were a mingled set
From town and field ; hand-workers in the arts,
Or at the spade and plough, while on them hung
A certain air of half-bred soldiery.
One, of thin face, and unheroic build,
Was grumbling somewhat at the turn of things,
When a huge man of muscle-twisted arms,
As one might get from labouring at a forge,
Shouted, "Whoever skulks from moving on
When the king orders 'March,'—why he's not worth
The liquor in this horn !" and down he turn'd

Its gaping mouth, from which, as twice his lips

Had pull'd at its contents, not a drop flow'd.

"I think," rejoin'd the other, "you're the same—

A year or so ago, at Winchester,—

Yes, you *are* he who threw at Ælfred's head

A log that did good service.   How much coin

Did the king price it at?"   "You hare-heart, you!"

Replied the smith ; "*you* weren't at Winchester.

And if you were, what, has your back got eyes?

Your face was surely furthest from the fight.

The king's a good man!"   "Pshaw!" rejoin'd the first.

"I tell thee," cried the other one in wrath,

"I come from Ripon, and King Athelstan

Hath richly dower'd a monastery there.

The hospital of Mary Magdalene

Adjoins it close, and round and round the church

A sanctuary spreads outwards for a mile.

A good man he who could do this, say I?"

So too his hearers said or seem'd to say.

"Yes," mutter'd his antagonist again,

" *You* doubtless found the sanctuary of use.

But if you live at Ripon, what a way

It was to come uncall'd to Winchester !"

" The hospital will cure you of the mange !"

Return'd the big man.   " Where's your loyalty ?"

"Where's Ethelwald ?" said he. " You skinny traitor !"

Thunder'd the smith.   " What matter where he is ?

We have a better man in Athelstan.

Who is the soldier's friend ?—why, Athelstan !

Who puts the nobles down, and gives the Church,

That takes the poor man's part, a lift on high ?

Who fights as if he loved it ?—Athelstan !

Who leads his men where plunder can be had,

Then shares the spoil 'mid all ?—King Athelstan !

What wouldst thou   more, thou   needle-threading

     slave ? "

   The latter fact had such authority,

Made weightier by raised arm, and voice that seem'd

To hammer it into the hearers' heads,

It took the breath from opposition,
If aught there was to fight such sentiments.

   So grew the wave of preparation
Blown up by valorous words, the wind of talk,
And swoll'n by floods from many a country spring,
Until its crest rose up exultingly,
Foam-tipp'd with rage, but not directionless,
And with an ominous murmur onward roll'd
Towards the limits of Northumbria.

BOOK II.

A SHIP was toiling in the shore-bound sea

That rolls between old England's dominant isle

And green Hibernia.   Narrow-form'd it was,

And with high scythe-like prow, that, as it dipp'd,

Mow'd down the frothy herbage of the waves.

Already to the sailor's eye appear'd,

Though distant yet, the vapour-sheeted hills

That with their rugged outlines tore the mist

And stood like gloomy giants at the side

Of deep-bay'd havens ; with a sideway course,

The ship work'd on its foamy way to land,

Slow, and finessing with the western wind.

Thus may a lover strive by tortuous arts,

And diplomatic turns of countenance,

And wise embarrassments of doubtful talk,

To take by stealth the virgin citadel

Of some proud beauty's heart, that won't be won

When it can see th' invader and th' advance.

Over the vessel's side there leant a youth,*

Who look'd into the waves with steady gaze,

As if he strove on their unruliness

To fix the motion of his will; but they

Who glanced into his face saw legibly

That his thoughts were not with the winds or waves,

Or with hard present things that to the brain

---

* When Sihtric had perished, his two sons, Guthforth and Anlaf, one with the propensities of a buccaneer, the other with the ambition of a king, took the courses traced out for them by the destiny of their natures. No two characters could be more strikingly unlike. History, when dealing with such persons, appears to be converted into romance, or thrown back into the heroic ages when men were actuated by motives now scarcely recognised as sources of human action. Guthforth's career, of which however we obtain but casual glimpses, is a poem in itself—his flight from Northumbria, his asylum in Scotland, his meditated surrender, his piratical life, his visit to the court of Athelstan, his preference of sea-roving to tame dependence, all these things impart a flush and a glow to the early history of England which gives it a striking resemblance to that of Hellas. Of Anlaf I shall speak further on.

Transmit their portraiture.   He thought (if such

Can be call'd thought, when past and future scour

With a long train of ghostly followers,

Of jumbled facts and possibilities,

Through the submissive mind), much then he thought

Of that foul day when he and Guthforth fled

Before the Saxons in Northumbria.

'Tis pity that brave men should fight in vain.

But of two combatants the losing one

May be the braver, and a loss like that

Be but a gain of honour and of fame,

And a pleased sense of having struggled much

For what is so much to be coveted ;

Of greater wisdom too, and keener hope

Of feeding one's ambition to the full

At the next feast which slaughter celebrates.

For brave was Anlaf, and right bravely risk'd

His royal blood to overwhelm the hosts

That to Northumbria brought the choice of war,

To fly, to die, or yield ; and oft he led

His followers, gather'd from the dreadful field

In warlike knots of men, which he unloosed,

Watching occasion, on the thinnest foe,

To spread destruction round, and desperate rout.

But with each rush of force, or politic snare,

Framed to entice aside and kill at ease,

There, like a Fate, was present Athelstan !

And, as the billows on a rock-arm'd shore,

So the fierce waves of battle broke in spray

Before the might of his compelling arm,

Before the wit of his soul's providence.

And Anlaf rush'd at danger, as if bent

To snatch a crown from out it, or to lose

All memory of its loss, but 'mid the storm

Of spears and arrows, and the clashing fall

Of sword and battle-axe, when all the air

Was dark with missiles, or confused with cries,

Unhurt amid the wreck he past, and, turning,

Saw his best friends lie stiff and passionless,

Never again to counsel him with words,

Never again to strike a blow for him,

And with large wounds, whose hideous gory mouths

Seem'd to cry out "This have we done for thee !

Hast thou yet better left than we, that life

Can keep thee from thy seat in Odin's hall,

Where Death will make thee free, if nobly dead !"

Thus as he stood despairing, and content

To be as one of those he look'd upon,

A Saxon warrior rush'd on him, and swung

His weapon at him, crying out "All hail,

Prince of Northumbria, King to come of Wessex !

Thus do I dub thee monarch !" and the blow

Bow'd Anlaf to his knees ; but, springing up

With vigour, which the suddenness and shame

Madden'd to fury, "Thus," he shouted, "I

Accept the omen and commence my reign !"

And, with a backward sweep of his long sword,
As the man past him overstretch'd by force
Of his own stroke, he cut the babbling head
Sheer off the shoulders.   As it fell to earth,
The boastful lips still moved as if in talk,
While on the scarce-dead features there yet dwelt
The look of valorous scorn, but on them soon
Darkness and silence dropt for evermore.

   Then Anlaf, in whose mind the heated blood
Had kindled new desires, was roused to hope,
And, turning from the dead, secured in life
A second chance for empire, and he fled
Far from the regions where his sire had reign'd.

   Nor was Prince Guthforth wanting in that day
Of bloody efforts.   With a dogged pow'r
He beat down those who would oppose his path,
Or sought to vex his rest when rest he sought.
But when he saw his brother Anlaf fly

From the lost field, he deem'd it profitless

His further presence there, and so he left ;

But took a different path, and turn'd his steps

To Scotland and the Court of Constantine.

There did he live some time as pleasantly

As his taste suffer'd, for he better loved

Than the land's flowery atmosphere to sniff

The pungent incense of the briny wave.

But, after months, there came to Constantine

A letter, full of counsel, kind and wise,

From Athelstan, the king and conqueror,

Which, when his wily host read, instantly

He sent to Guthforth, warning him that those

Who sought his person were abroad, so he,

For his own good, would shut him up at home.

Then Guthforth was not wrath, but shrugg'd himself,

Crying, " I wonder how much Scotland gets

For selling me to England !   'Tis a change,

And may be not the last.—My lady-love !

Poor thing !   She'll weep her eyes out at the news.

They say that tears are salt."   Then lay he down,
Willing to wait, and thinking of the sea.

    And now the ship where Anlaf sat had work'd
Its weary way within clear sight of shore.
Rugged it was, and coldly prominent
With treeless mountains, and indented nests,
Which the sea made itself betwixt the hills.
Straight for a vale the vessel steer'd between
Two guardian heads, tall pillars at the horns
Of a great bay, whose ample curvature
Had room to shelter from pursuing winds
The ships of Denmark trebly told and more.
From out its breast three islands rose, which check'd
The forward waves that roll'd like riotous guests
To break the quiet of a sleeping house.

    And Anlaf in that island found a home,
Growing his pow'r for years, and won himself
A small dominion for immediate want,

Help'd by his brother Danes who cluster'd there.

But never did the lost Northumbria pass

From out his memory, and beyond e'en this

The vision of a greater kingdom rose.

So, drop by drop, he mass'd the elements

Of war and enmity to Athelstan ;

Thus by a dam the waters are heap'd up

From many a rill, led down from many a source,

Until, the check removed, the dangerous flood

Bursts in its aggregated might, to wreck

The industry of pastures and of fields.

York's castle had changed masters, and within

Oft was the banquet set for Athelstan.

And, like a king attired, there sat the king.

Dark-blue his cloak, and warmly delicate,

Hung from his shoulders ; soft it was, and gleam'd

With its broad golden binding as he turn'd.

His inner coat was crimson, deeply-toned,

And loosely fitting to the stalwart form.

E

His dark-brown hose, like a rich garden-bed,
Grew silver flowers, and from his regal brow,
'Mid his thick ringlets, rose a small thin crown,
Like a dwarf turret miniatured in gold.

Time on his face had deeply character'd
The sense of his position,—there was there
Knowledge of strengthen'd pow'r, and stern resolve
To hold the gain though Europe should gainsay.
Yet with a restless look, that spoke the love
Of doing something, rather than to sit
In one's own chamber communing with self,
And asking questions asked too easily.

Bare was the ample banquet-hall where sat
The Saxon warriors, for the savage Dane
Was savage in his tastes, nor yet had learnt
The arts of peace ; the luxuries of the eye ;
Gradations of proportion'd magnitudes ;
And various colours wedded happily.

Space mark'd with strength the features of the Hall,

Space for a friend to feast within, and strength

To keep a foe without it.   Saxon polish

Had stretch'd a cloth on the stout board that bore

The weight of viands, where great flesh of deer

Shared the day's honours with more general swine.*

Nor wanted there the dairy's harmless fruits,

And the sweet products of the patient bee.

Large cups of beaten gold convey'd rich wine

To noble lips, while others sat and quaff'd

With equal relish from the humble horn

Ripe ale and mead.   And equal was the zest

---

* Our ancestors were scarcely more remarkable for anything than for their passion for feeding on pork. Swine shared the island with them, and indicated, perhaps, to themselves the fairer portion of it, the woods, the fens, the forests, where they roamed like gentlemen, attended by troops of valets. Philosophers may perhaps discover in the prevalence of this peculiar diet one cause of that absence of refinement which marked their manners. Stalwart and vigorous they were, but withal somewhat coarse and sensual; much given to drinking, and in their treatment of women anything but chivalrous. The drinks with which they washed down their pork were strong ale, mead, and wine, heated and spiced, the more readily to inflame their blood; yet they protracted their feasts during several days, probably until they had completely blunted their appetites, and required a considerable period of repose to qualify them for renewing the conflict.

Wherewith the Thane, and he of lower rank

Who follow'd where his betters led, and fought

When his lord bid him fight, in half-drunk tones—

All happy thus 'till they should fight again—

Scream'd out their joy for the great victory

Won by the Saxon English o'er the Dane,

And which to Wessex bound Northumbria

In firmer bonds than those that, fancy-burst,

Tied Sihtric to the bed of Eadgitha.

The sun was high in heaven one autumn day

When 'mid the general voices of the feast

And the long fumes of brain-confounding wine,

A man without sought audience of the king :

And when before the Saxon prince he stood

Less in his height he seem'd, and less in years.

Coarse-framed he was and beaten by the winds,

And burnish'd by the sun ; nor did his dress

Betray the hand of one whom leisured taste

Had deck'd to turn into a drawing-room

To be admired by peaceful coxcombry.

More like a fighting man by land or sea

He did appear, whom haste forbade to change

His toil-worn cloak, as all unarm'd he stood

Before the king, yet wanted not the look

Which drew attention to him, though unfurnish'd

With trappings of defence or ornament.

" Thy mission and thy name ! " quoth Athelstan.

" My mission to seek pardon from a foe,

(And I shall find it, if a generous one,)

And my name Guthforth ! " thus replied the Dane.

Then the king question'd him with steady gaze,

But not again with words ; and when his mind

Was settled into act, " Here find," he cried,

" A freer home-berth than with Scotland's king.

How didst thou baffle thy friend's kind compulsion

That would have made thee come unwillingly

Where thy bold willingness hath made thee welcome ?"

" Nay !" said the blunt-speech'd Dane, " to tell the

  arts

Which loosed me from the hold of Constantine,
Might, by great Odin, hazard their success
On the next chance of like occasion."
Then the king, smiling, " Rest thee, noble Dane,
Long as thou wilt, and find a roof secure
From the rough weather, and a well-spread board.
Though stormy weather little vexeth thee,
If what men say be true, that thou hast reign'd
A predatory sovereign of the seas
Since quitting Scottish hospitality."
And the king look'd him over, as a book
That is look'd over by some learned man
Who can alone make out its character;
While Guthforth, lounging to a vacant seat,
Seized the next cup, and filling it with drink
" To this last change of life, and may it thrive!"
He drank, and humm'd a sea-tune carelessly.

And day by day the king conversed with Guth-
    forth,

To bind him to him by good offices,

And daily Guthforth drank with Athelstan,

Who talk'd to him of York, and how he needed

A tributary Prince as President

Of his demesnes in that vicinity;

And how 'twould be fair measure that a son

Of its late Prince should be its Prince again

With a changed title.   But the ears of Guthforth

Were somewhat dull to what his heart desired not.

Then spake he in return, and spake of Anlaf,

Of Anlaf's many virtues, strangely form'd

To reach to the extreme necessities

That lie 'twixt peace and war; whose voice could
          hurl,

With its inspiriting shout, a hundred men

Against a thousand, in a hopeful fight,

Or could unravel a self-woven song,

And use its threads to snare a maiden's ear.

But Athelstan thought Anlaf's tastes too large

To be shut up within Northumbria;

So said to Guthforth, "Why, thy brother rules
A principality of Irishmen,
And plots and plans with Scandinavian heads,
In order that his own be crown'd in London ;
But, if the path 'twixt scheming and success
Were pass'd by him in safety, would he halve
His power with thee—with one so near in blood
As is a brother ? Our own relatives
Stand oft on their relationship itself
To reach their hands out to strange liberties."
And Guthforth heard him speak, but not convinced
Took a long draught to clear his brain, and sat
In sleepy meditation discontent.
For much the peaceful tameness of the Court
Weigh'd on his restless spirit, and he long'd
Again to lead the free life of the sea,
Free for himself and crew, to take their choice
Of goods where'er they landed, ravaging
Life and life's chattels, leaving in exchange
The terror of their names.   To ease his heart,

Heavy with absence, he would sometime sing
Of what he loved in rugged harmony.

A horse, a horse for me !
My soul's on fire to ride ;
My ship at sea
The horse shall be,
And, away on the roaring tide !
Then saddle for me
My ship at sea,
And I'm off on the roaring tide !

My rudder's the rein wherewith
I'll guide this noble steed ;
And the driving wind
Like a spur behind
Shall urge it on to speed.
In the driving wind
A spur I'll find,
For the flanks of my foaming steed.

Ha ! ha ! I am mounted now
O'er the waves that beneath me bend,

And before my face
Spreads out the space
Of Ocean, without end !
'Tis a glorious race
O'er Ocean's space,
To fly and to find no end !

Strong was the castle which th' encroaching Dane
Had built at York ; yet Athelstan thought fit
To lay its masses level with the soil,
In place of turning, when the Dane was out,
The foe's defences 'gainst th' offensive foe.

Round-shaped it was, and, raised upon a keep,
A strong thick wall embraced it like a friend
To keep from harm the soldiers housed within.
A deep ditch compass'd all, and, edging this,
A palisaded mound of beaten earth,
Upon whose back a lofty wall arose
Like an imperial safeguard turreted.

As each thick bulwark fell before the rage

Of demolition, many a nook laid bare

To greedy eyes its precious hiding-bed

Where gold lay couch'd, and stones outvaluing gold.

Great was the noise of plundering soldiery

Rushing from spot to spot, as if they grudged

The present pillage which delayed the time

From entering on the future.   Joy it was

To thunder at some oaken chest that held

A treasure all unknown, but all their own,

While the keen look watch'd, gambler-like, a stake

Sure to turn prize without a blank to lose.

For rich the harvest heap'd of various spoil

Which the sea-kings had reap'd impartially,

From church or cottage, noble Thane or churl.

The silver altar-cloth that form'd a soil

For flowers of gold to bloom on ; or large bracelet,

The prize of valour from a warrior's wrist ;

Or gem-bright brooch, or neck-lace that had shone

On England's swan-neck'd daughters, all were shared

In hot division by the sturdy hands

That had help'd Athelstan to oust the Dane.

For the king, politicly generous,*

Cried to his soldiers " Welcome to the prey !

All help themselves as best they like !" and each

Did help himself as he liked best in full.

And when hands could not hold, the tunic, loop'd

Into a hollow, supplemented them ;

And Guthforth stood and saw the sight and cried

(For his rough nature did not want for wit)

" What a king gives a king may take again !"

And monarchs then were not the things they are

In these degenerate times, when sons receive

---

* One of the first strokes of Athelstan's policy noticed by historians, was the distribution among his soldiers of the Danish treasures found in York Castle. No doubt the act was judicious, but the demolition of the fortress in which the spoil was found, betokened quite as signal a want of policy. Athelstan's father had laboured throughout his whole reign to make England bristle with strong places, and Athelstan, affecting to be able to dispense with them, displayed an inferiority of judgment which must have become apparent even to the least discerning, when he found himself under the necessity of purchasing the services of the northern Buccaneer, and thus commencing that system which lasted till the battle of Hastings.

From their mild parents an unfought-for crown.

Some few days thence a soldier sought the king,

And craved for justice, crying, that he sold

For a mean price a costly ornament

Of beaten gold, triangularly curved,

Set with projecting knobs, from each of which

Hung a pure string of pearls, from first to last

Gaining in beauty as they grew in size.

This did he sell to some sagacious Thane,

And as the price was light when weigh'd against

The worth of the thing sold, he sought redress

For the wrong practised on his ignorance.

Thereon an angry pleasure lit the eyes

Of Athelstan, and next day summoning

The Thane, he bade him bring the ornament—

Arrived, the king cried "Truly beautiful!

Fix not a royal price on it, and we

Will buy it of thee." Answer'd then the Thane,

"A merchant-pedlar, who, when purchasing,

Deals not in royal prices, such a one

Hath offer'd me ten golden pieces for it ;"

Smiling, the king exclaim'd, "Stand forth !" and quick

Stood forth the soldier from his hiding-place ;

When to the troubled Thane spake Athelstan—

" Keep thou one piece to reimburse thy pains,

And give this man nine golden pieces, now ;

Next, I advise thee, find the pedlar out,

And keep him to his offer !"   Gladly off

The soldier ran, and grasping in his hand

The first sum six times told ; and gladly off

The noble walk'd, content to be so school'd,

And nothing sharper, by the warrior-king.

And all men spoke the praise of Athelstan;

And how he would not the least wrong be done,

Under the cover of fortuitous birth,

To the least man who served his country well.

   Again the feast was set, and Athelstan

Look'd round upon the chiefs that sat there, lords

Of council and of war; but saw he none

By nature dower'd more largely than himself,

None there so great as he; for God had made

The war to fly before him, and had bid

His counsels, aim'd from far, make centre hits

In what they flew at; yet had left that look,

Half-anxious, on his gracious lineaments,

Such as the brave might wear, who fear, tho' brave,

Being sensitive, lest they be thought to fear.

But as his eye roam'd o'er the chieftains round,

One was not there who had been used to come—

Prince Guthforth, ever constant to the wine;

Yet the wise king said nothing, and he drank,

And made his nobles drink, and wash'd away

The marks of care-thought, brightening to the feast

In talk and laughter more than was his wont.

But when the night was thick, alone he sought

His chamber, and there mapp'd the future out,

Heated with dreams of possibilities,

The visions of the great not great enough.

Hindrance he cared not for—the very work
Of overcoming was itself a joy.
Then came his sister Eadgitha, and look'd
Demurely handsome ; to her Athelstan,
"What doth my sister here ?"   Then she, "I crave
Permission to impart my purposes.
I'm tired of greatness, if one can be tired
Of what was never relish'd.   I would wish
To hide myself from life and from the world
Within some holy abbey."   "So !" return'd
The king, "And leave the world to help itself,
Withdrawing one more labourer from the work
That all should handle !"   "Yet," said Eadgitha,
"If all would thus renounce its vanities,
The world would want no being set to rights
When nothing there went wrong."   Then Athelstan :
"My sister ! vanity's a curious plant,
That grows in cloisters as in palace-courts.
Let that alone.   Suppose mankind retired,
Shut up in idle inoffensiveness,

Soon would some few ambitious souls emerge

From out the mass, to plot, and seize, and slay

For their own good, and make confusion worse,

As finding all things open to their use,

And the great world's securities unlock'd !"

"I do my duty,—that," said Eadgitha,

"Should be enough for me :—what others do,

Let them who do it answer it themselves !"

"But *is* it thus thy duty, sister mine !"

Cried Athelstan, "to fly a general law ?

All nature works, and every living thing

In its vocation seems ordain'd to move

In ceaseless interchange of toil and pause,

The pause alone to husband strength for toil.

Only in Heav'n is perfect rest ; the way

To get there is through weariness on earth."

"Nay brother !" replied Eadgitha, "thyself

Art not an instance the best possible

Of work made happy.   Thou hast labor'd well.

How long is it since Exe and Tamar saw,

Expell'd by thee, the Western Britons fly,
And Saxon rule hold all of Exeter —
Which thou didst roundly fence with walls and towers,
And all the surety possible in stone?
As saplings bow before the blast, so bent
The Princes of the Welsh at Hereford;
And to prevent thy victories breaking up
Their name and nation, brought their subject gifts,
Silver and gold enough to arm a host;
And hounds and falcons taught to hunt their prey
O'er hill and dale, and through the fields of air.
Is't not enough? And wilt thou ne'er eschew
These wars and storms, and sun thyself in peace?
Or is the joy in *getting*, not in got?
Ambition too sees not what others see,—
The want of cleanness in its instruments."

"Nay!" returned Athelstan, but thoughtfully.
"If perfect means be waited for to help
The good upon its way, 'twill ne'er o'ertake

The evil that is strong, and runs before."—
Then did he break off mutteringly, and seem'd
Brain-clouded, wrapt in speculative mists;
And Eadgitha went off and made no sound
In going, save a small decorous sigh.

King Athelstan sat silent for awhile,
And like a statue, save the play of thought
Over the fair ground of his countenance;
Then, starting from his dream, cried " Summon
　　　　Eldred ! "
And Eldred the cup-bearer came at call.
A prudent man, nor unaccustomed he
To share the secrets of the royal heart.
Noble he was by birth, by nature brave :
This last a quality not always found
Conjoin'd with the smooth tongue's obsequiousness.
But thus he loved to work his purposes
(Using an instrument he well could use)
By sidelong and suggestive flattery :

As may a ship approach by tortuous course,

The land in view, and nearing with each tack

The distant object which it seems to fly.

" Elfred !" exclaimed the king, " more oft this day

Than others hast thou mix'd the cup for me,

But, little comfort mingled with the draught.

Guthforth hath fled, thou see'st—when, wherefore—

     where ?"

" And what is Guthforth to my royal lord,

That Athelstan should mind so small a man ?"

Cried Eldred ; and then answer'd Athelstan,

" He is the son of Sihtric the dead king,

Whose kingdom we have taken ;—brother, too,

To Anlaf who is, (if some Irish bog

Have not in kindness drown'd him) yet alive.

So Guthforth, small himself, when leagued with others,

May swell their greatness—yet he's changeable."

" He hath but gone," cried Eldred, " to his own—

He cannot live without his element,

And gasps for water.   Such sea-monsters walk

Less dangerous on the land."   Then Athelstan :

" But he can leave his floating den to vex

Our fruitful coasts with his unquiet teeth,

Tearing the life and bearing off the prey.

So can he bring in his land-cursèd ships

Some thousand wolves of Scandinavian breed

To hunt our flocks where Anlaf bids him loose.

Yet am I wrong to waste my thoughts on him—

I am not well to-night ; my brain is hot.

It is the curse of pow'r, that they who raise

The building up, can ne'er relax their toil

Adding new props to stay the edifice."

" They say the tallest pillar may be shaken,"

Quoth Eldred, " by the fingers of a child ;

So men may shake thy pow'r, but not o'erturn.

Ay ! he were rash indeed who would undo

What thou hast done for England—would recal

The greatness thou hast giv'n it !"   Athelstan,

Starting, as from a sudden prick of fire,

More earnestly than was his wont—at least

Than he was wont to show his heart abroad,—
Cried, "Say again—England is growing great.
And have not I watch'd, foster'd all its growth?
Heav'n too is great, and will not strictly scan
The necessary means that lead to good—
Will not with its avenging hatred smite
Detail'd injustice, when the end is just.
When one hath raised a nation to a height
It never knew of glory and of joy,
Shall individual wrongs, small harshnesses,
Obtrude their censure, and confound the whole,
Crying out, 'Look at us!' and with blind eye
To the diffused advantage, damn the man
Who makes a million blest?" "Not so, your Grace!"
Cried Eldred. "If the good men do mankind
Must wait the perfect means to carry it
Unto the end it seeks, the world may sleep
In the last night when all the stars go out
Before it reach the goal." Then Athelstan :
" Well, well; when Power affects to do great good,

It is the curse of our humanity,

Passion, and chance, and circumstance step in

And intercept the aim.   Thou say'st that I

Have raised this England up beyond herself,

And I would lift her higher ; but for this

I must have room to wield my instruments

Of mind or muscle, that they freely fall

Where I shall choose, nor meet opposing force

To break their incidence."   "'Tis true, my lord !"

Said Eldred, " Sad and true.   The best designs

Are often thwarted by the best.   The good,

When high in rank, and favorites with the crowd,

May do most ill ——" and here the cup-bearer

Glanced at the countenance of Athelstan,

And saw that it was darker than at first.

" I wait," the king replied, " tho' hard to wait,

Till Heav'n destroy the yet unripe designs

Of those whose murmurs are, ' The throne is fill'd

By the chance child of illegitimate love '—

Tho' for his country's good legitimately,

Not for himself, but her, he wields its power."

" Prince Edwin," whisper'd Eldred, " What of him ?"

Impetuously cried Athelstan,—" My lord,

He is your brother !" and the royal face

Grew darker still as spake the cup-bearer.

" He is of princely birth, and widely loved ;

Should such a man do ill, wer't wise to screen

The wrong behind the royalty ?"   The king

Was silent ; and on went the cup-bearer,

" Let me remind your Grace, that England asks

Her greatness from yourself, and will not brook

The loss of the least glory to her name,

Lost by the weakness of a private love."

" What would'st thou ?" said the king, and in a tone

As if he ask'd no answer : then there came

A boding pause, a silence terrible,

As if thought shrunk from words, as ghosts to thrust

Their unsubstantial horrors on the light.

And in the stillness Athelstan's great sword,

Missing its prop against an oaken seat,

Broke like a thunder-crash upon the floor.

The monarch started at the sound ; but he,

The venturous Eldred, smiled, and started not.

Again spake Eldred slowly with soft voice,

"I have a charge of capital consequence

Against ——" but Athelstan sprang up and cried

"Not yet!" and strode about the room, as struggling

To gain a hardness to hear anything—

"A charge of capital consequence," he cried,

Returning, "against whom?" and Eldred answer'd,

"Against a Prince—thy princely brother Edwin!" *

* The sophistry by which Athelstan sought to disguise from himself
the heinousness of his attempt against his brother Edwin, is by no
means unfamiliar to tyrants. Crime as crime, naked and unblushing,
is revolting to the worst of men. Deeds of guilt are habitually
preceded by a process of Jesuitical logic, which converts the intended
victim into an enemy, and steeps the hands in falsehood before they
are crimsoned by assassination. How far Athelstan's cup-bearer
may have aided in lulling his conscience to sleep is uncertain ; but
tradition attributes to him, perhaps unjustly, a large share of the
king's criminality, though it be far from uncommon to find about an
unscrupulous monarch, men eager, and even willing, to forestall his
worst wishes. Some writers have affected scepticism regarding this
portion of Athelstan's career, but the remorse and penance described

And when the king heard what he thought to hear,

Yet shook he—he who never shook in fight,

As if some giant thought had seized on him

And wrench'd his stalwart frame with all its force,

While he with all his force too strove to keep

His body still, but could not—then, at length,

He ask'd, "But hast thou proof?" "Best proof," cried
          Eldred.

"Else could I dare to grieve your Grace, and charge

Your Grace's brother?" "Brother!" cried the king,

And turn'd his head half sideways, as he sat

Fronting the light, and with his large hand hid

The thoughts that knit his brow.   If Eldred saw

His face more pale when he unclosed again

The curtain of his fingers, 'twas perchance

by Mr. St. John would be motiveless unless springing from the con-
sciousness of some portentous effort of villany.   "The crime having
been perpetrated," says the writer, "remorse seized upon the mind
of the king, who, believing like an Indian ascetic in the efficacy of
torture, condemned himself to a seven years' penance, which only
closed with his life.   By way moreover of further expiation, he is said
to have put to death the cup-bearer, who had artfully fanned his
hatred against his brother."—"History of the four Conquests of
England," vol. i. p. 340.

The tint of pity for his brother's fate :

And he said, " If it must—this sacrifice—

God help me—I'm too weak to be a king—

Proof, didst thou say, unquestion'd proof?" " My lord !

Unquestion'd proof !" return'd the cup-bearer.

Then said the king, " Now go.   Thou canst not think

I love not mercy;—see that thou have proof.

Earth hath not pains to damn thee half enough

If thou dar'st lay aught rashly to the charge

Of the great Alfred's grandson— and now go !"

And without word or gesture Eldred went.

Then as King Athelstan was tired, and turn'd

To seek his rest, and musing as he went,

Paced down the narrow passage, Eadgitha,

From a low room that border'd on his way,

Hymn'd a sad hymn, and thus he heard her sing :—

      Vanity—O vanity !

      Who would live when he could die ?

Weak our hearts, but Hell is strong;
Short our years, but Death is long;
Then the best life to be led
Is where living seem like dead.

Riches rot, and glory flies,
Pleasure droops, and vigour dies.
Monarch's crown and cowl of monk
Down to the same dust have sunk;
Then or all, from king to slave,
The best dwelling is the grave.

When did age find ever truth
In the promises of youth?
Joy and hope too fade away—
Bury them while yet 'tis day.
Wherefore wait until the night?
Hide both them and us from sight.

And the king thought to smile, but only frown'd;
Then as he walk'd down the long corridor,
Low-roof'd, and unadorn'd, and strong enough
To keep all enemies but one without,

His footsteps through the vaulted stillness rang

Upon the naked floor.   The lamps o'erhead

Were struggling for a little more of life,

Flashing alternate streaks of light and shade

Upon the walls, and hissing their last sounds

Before the darkness and the silence came.

BOOK III.

Now England had begun to spread abroad

The branches of her glory ; for at home

There was the root of confidence—a sense

That he who ruled them, vigilantly loved

The honour of the ruled ; a soil indeed

Most fit to grow dominion.   The broad seas

That lash'd her empire had a prouder curl

Frothing around the shores, where greater strength

Was bred from greater union ; where weak men

Had merg'd their being in a man more strong ;

And pass'd their pow'r—which, like a mischievous child,

Could break, and unmake rulers without skill

To piece the damage—into firmer hands.

A king, as seventh, is better, e'en tho' bad,

G

Than six small princes who have made him up,
And who with interacting hatred reign'd
Each for himself and ruin for the rest.

    The seas indeed were proud, yet cruelty
May go with pride, for cruelly they rose
On a small boat that on a cheerless day
Stagger'd and groan'd as if it shrank in pain
From dissolution on its watery bed.
Oarless and sailless, it was driven on
Directionless, at mercy of the things
That have no mercy, and within it sat
Two cold despairing men, no better furnish'd
Than was the boat that bore them; she without
The means of art to steer a willing course,
They unsupplied with natural food or drink
To make life tenable. The older man
Was armour-bearer to the youth who touch'd
His side, and he the grandson of a king.
Toss'd helplessly, they drifted; sad it is

To die by any fate in manhood's spring,

But sadder still to be the jest of death,

Without the pow'r to fight the hands that snatch

Dear life away before our desperate eyes.

And as a lion dashes at a bait

Within the barr'd enclosure of a cage,

And strives to rend the thick defence of wood

That shuts the kid from his insatiate jaws ;

So roar'd the waters on th' unhappy pair,

Shaking their feeble tenement, and raised

Their foamy heads above its sides, and look'd

Impatient on the prey they coveted.

Wildly the armour-bearer stampt, and threw

His brawny arms aloft and ask'd if Heav'n

Had no more justice than its subject earth—

Then gnash'd his raging teeth, and cursed the king :

And if his wishes had had potency

They would have risen in mad rebellion

And given a thousand deaths to Athelstan.

For this the youth was Edwin ; he who sat

With his still hopeless look ; and then anon

It wore an eager flush, as if he thought

That instant to rush downward to his doom.

For Eldred, the king's cup-bearer, had brought

Charges of wickedness against the Prince,

And wicked charges, such strange wickedness

As the mere handling of it by the mind

Would leave a soil behind—yet wanted not

Consenting tongues to swear to the bad truth,

Whatever might be the heart's evidence.

And so the judges, honourable men,

Prompt to do justice, e'en to work their office

Upon the person of a Prince, condemn'd

Young Edwin to this watery penalty.

And this they call'd "Heaven's judgment"—to be

        thrown

Into the arms of the unjudging sea,

To crush or cast upon the naked shore ;

A challenge to the God of all to say

His sentence on the right or wrong ; a plan
Whereby man calls upon Omniscience
To do his duty for him when it chafes.

And Edwin rose, and wrang his hands, and cried
" Lo ! this is Guthforth's element ! This sea
That howls upon the helpless way-farer.
Is this the pleasant slave that bears his lord
On the curved convoy of his stormy back
To conquest and to joy ? Then why are we
So toss'd and plagued by its rebellious waves,
And stretch'd at by their white and billowy jaws ?—
Ha ! what an insolent cruelty it is
Thus to have ever-present to our eyes
The instruments of death before we die ? "

For Guthforth, at the court of Athelstan,
Though rude by nature, nor much given to speech,
Had form'd a friendship with a second soul,
Attracted by its opposite, for mild

Was Edwin in his outward lineaments

And gentle in his yearnings, tho' with spirit

That could uphold the right, when strongly shown,

Yet bore with wrong awhile, and deem'd it right

Rather than strive with opposition

To extricate the truth : the king's own brother,

Younger in years, but born of lawful love,

His courteous ways, and rightly royal blood

Had made him more belov'd by the king's subjects

Than by the king.   And Guthforth talk'd with him,

And with rude tongue, yet picturesque in phrase,

Such as men use when they describe the treasure

Where their heart lies, he spake of the great sea,

And of its manifold magnificence ;

Its glassy vastness when the storm-king sleeps

Beneath its surface in some oozy cave,

Until he wake, and his broad shoulders heave

The level plain up, and confound the prospect

Broken to multitudinous mountain-tops.

Then, to rush onward as the ocean-steed

Spreads its white pinions to the screaming wind,

And o'er the vallied billows, and the hills,

Flies, with heel scattering foam like dust, and leaves

Undented its illimitable course.

This listening to the young Prince long'd to tempt

The new delights of the unstable sea,

And had he not stood near a throne on land,

He might have wish'd, in place of living people,

To rule the fierce republic of the waves.

  And still upon the inhospitable sea

The unwilling travellers found no hope nor rest ;

The red sun lower'd at them the whole long day,

And kept down sinking nearer to his end,

As they to theirs ; this was the only change

That colour'd their monotony of fate.

Next the night fell upon them, but the sea

Knew no remissness night or day, but beat

Ever on this death's cradle, in the which

Were rudely rock'd these two despairing lives,

And the old armour-bearer sat, and watch'd

By Edwin as he lay, and muttering gazed

Into the ocean, as if questioning

Its right to torture him ; at last his eyes,

Tired with his own and his lord's sorrow, closed

In a short blessed quiet, and he slept.

And then he dreamt that in the royal house,

One day as he was kneeling to the king,

The crown fell off the head of Athelstan,

And, wounding him, roll'd onward to the feet

Of Edwin, who was near, when he, tho' grazed

But slightly by the dangerous diadem,

Fell to earth headlong, and lay there as dead.

Waking, he saw the prince rise up and spring

From the boat's side into the deadly sea.

With a great cry the old man rose, and threw

His hands straight out, but only grasp'd the air ;

Then knelt and peer'd into the deep dark grave,

And watch'd and watch'd, and, with short interval,

Close by his eyes the body floated up—

By the right arm he seized it, dragging it
Into the boat, whose weighted edge bowed low
Beneath the waters.   Vainly did he chafe
The dripping limbs, in vain call out the name
Of his loved master; and when broke the day
He saw a face on which in mournful lines
Was written, that for earthly sympathies
And earth's ambitions; for his own intents
Or for another's fears; for ill or good,
Prince Edwin, Edward's son, himself the son
Of Alfred the great king, had ceased to be.

Alone on the unsympathising sea
The armour-bearer's undirected course
Was held from hour to melancholy hour.
The wind had gone to sleep, but not the waves,
Which in vast swell resistless raised the boat
Upon their tops, then dragg'd it down again
To the dark hollow where themselves had sunk.
Alone on the unsympathising sea

He would have kill'd himself, but could not leave

The body of his lord again to drop

Into the jaws of that curs'd element.

At length a wind came stretching from the East,

And drove the sea before it ; wave met wave

In frothy conflict, but the wind was strong,

And turn'd the billows landward, till they cast

The live and dead upon the coast of Kent.

On the rough shore the faithful follower

Was roughly thrown, but never loosen'd hold

Of his dead lord ; and there on English soil,

With his bruised hands, and never-weary love,

Scoop'd for him a rude grave, and stampt the earth

Over the brother of King Athelstan.*

Hungry and faint, he then his sorrowful steps

Turn'd toward the inner land.   The sun rose high ;

* Matthew of Westminster, in a confused and rambling way, tells the story of Edwin's assassination and interment, A.D. 934. Simeon of Durham, p. 154, merely relates that Athelstan ordered his brother to be drowned in the sea. Upon the whole there seems no good reason, either for doubting the crime, or the manner in which it was perpetrated.

And on, and on he walk'd; but the long way
Wore out his hope of life; and down he sat,
Thinking no more to talk with other men.
Just then the pitying breeze bore to him sounds
Of distant merriment—again the wish
Of mixing with the living roused some strength
To seek the spot within his feeble limbs.
There a rude scene of customary joy
Was being acted; men and women danced
About the heathenish similitude
Of some old god or goddess, or the powers
That watch the crops, and overlook the fruits,
And mete their measure out to labouring men.
With less of grace than heartiness, they romp'd
In gay disorder round the effigy,
And sung or shouted forth a doggrel song.

Master and man are glad;
Work finish'd, and weather shining.
Where drink is free to be had,
What's the use of declining?

When a good wage is proffer'd,
    Who would be long in choosing?
And when a kiss is offer'd,
    What's the use of refusing?

If a law's bad when tried,
    Better is then the breaking it—
And if a kiss be denied,
    What's the harm of taking it?

Then all at once burst forth a noisy fray

Of chased and chasers ; and sharp fights when caught,

And shrieks and laughter and resounding lips.

A special group was rolling on the soil,

Confused in a fierce scramble of delight,

When like a stealthy spectre o'er them stood

The armour-bearer—gaunt, and ragged, pale,

Rough-hair'd, and bloody-eyed—quick horror seized

Both men and women there, and some on knees,

And some recumbent as if fixed in stone,

Gazed on that haggard face, that like a blight,

Descending on the bud and on the bloom,
Struck pleasure dead.   And long it was before
The armour-bearer, with his piteous tale
Of hard realities and human wants,
Dispersed their fears and gain'd their sympathy.

Time past, and England grew with it, for great
She was with friends and foes, and " Athelstan "
Became a name of growth proportionate ;
And were the greatness such that happiness
Held back, unable to keep pace with it,
'Twas from the cares that sprang to crowd the day
With occupation, and set loose the thoughts
That should at midnight fold themselves in rest.
So when the night had past its middle term
The king was wakeful—sleep and restlessness
Alternated in such uneasy change,
That it were hard to say which state was sleep
And which its want ; and ever in his ears,
Waking or dreaming, rose incessantly

The wintry hubbub of an open sea.

He grasp'd the bed, and shook the thick-carved oak

Of its supports, and, starting, with bare foot

Stamp'd on the solid earth, and walk'd and lay,

But found no rest ; for ever in his ears,

Waking or dreaming, rose incessantly

The wintry hubbub of an open sea.

And birds and beasts of bad presentiment,

That own'd no fond allegiance to a king,

Hover'd and flutter'd round the royal house,

And with a narrow and a wheezing cry,

As if the claw of hunger pinch'd their throats,

Answer'd, with most unmusical response,

The clamours of th'imaginary waves.

Pale rose the king from the ungracious night

To find no less disloyal was the day,

And men remark'd, nor envied, with what weight

The cares of empire prest the regal brow.

One morn the king rose early up from where

He had not rested ; for his thoughts were full

Of Edwin—Edwin and the open sea,

And the rude boat, unvictuall'd and unsteer'd.

" Doth Edwin live ?" and " Would he were alive !"

If such the monarch's thoughts, most heavily

They weigh'd upon his brain, and thence convey'd

To the fair face the lines of ceaseless pain.

" A way-worn man craves audience of the king."

Such the report that, made to Athelstan,

Drew an unthinking answer "let him come !"

And on his breast down sank the weary head.

But when he rais'd his eyes, they grew upon

A tall grim man who stood erect and still,

Batter'd, and scarr'd by work, and age, and grief,

With half defiant, half-reproachful look.

And the King look'd on him as if the grave

Had cast him up, or the deep-bottom'd sea,

For in his ancient face he recognised

Prince Edwin's armour-bearer.—" Thou alone !

Lives he yet ?   Thou alone !" cried Athelstan.

"I am alone!" he said, and even he

Pitied the look of blank heart-palsy, spread

O'er the king's face, and, like a dwarf that beards

A giant, over-powering all the power

And all the pride of that majestic man.

Still did he sit awhile, then motioning

For speech, again the armour-bearer spake.

"He died!   But not Heav'n's judgment slew my lord,

But his own act.   I buried him in Kent;

And now I live—I would that I were dead!"

The monarch heard, and went o'er instantly

From grief to passion, such a rage as fills

The bosom of the storm-king when he rends

With his red bolts the thick-ribb'd oaks that grow,

The forest tenants of a thousand years.

Swift, to his feet up-springing he exclaim'd,

"Heav'n kill'd him not, but false conspiracy—

Then shall the man who slew himself be slain—

Off—and bid Eldred come," and Eldred came;

But the high look of incens'd royalty

Fell somewhat lower, as it met the gaze

Of Eldred the cupbearer, who spake out

'Ere he was spoken, for he knew his doom.

" I *charged* Prince Edwin with a crime—no more—

The men who heard the proofs, and raised their votes

In condemnation, they are my defence

And their own judges—"   But then Athelstan

Broke in upon him with outcrying tongue

And passionate gesture more than was his wont,

For he contain'd himself within himself,

And held his feelings curb'd, lest they should shake

His steadiness of prospect, or abate

The reverence due to outward majesty,

" Words come at will to justify the deeds

Of every traitor—rid the land of this !"

" A few more words !" cried Eldred, and he spake

In a soft clear-voiced tone, as erst he spake

Counselling the king upon that fatal night,

" Edwin is dead.   And I myself shall soon

Be nothing more than unimpassion'd clay,

H

Yet there are two who may revenge me yet ;

Anlaf, and thy own conscience, Athelstan !"

The king replied not, signalling to lead

The speaker off, who show'd nor hope nor fear.

And when the day was done—the warm bright day—

And the chill night hour came, the wife of Eldred

Went silent to her widow'd bed ; her children

Cried for their father's kiss, but found it not."

Time sped, and still "How great is Athelstan !

Cried all men, for he made his country stand

Erect among the nations.   To her shores

Came all whom change of creed or politics,

Or unsuccessful meddling with the ways

Of serving God, or ruling men, or chance

Without a cause, or popular jealousies,

Or despots and their doubts, had forced to fly

The vital risk of living where they loved,

And seek abroad the home not found at home.*

* Sir Francis Palgrave, in his "History of Normandy and

Yet did not this content king Athelstan;

His thoughts seem'd ever wandering forth, at least

When not detain'd by strong and present need,

In search of something which they sought in vain.

And therefore sent he for a holy man,

To counsel, and to fix a penance on him,

A seven years' penance for his many sins,

And for young Edwin's death—and was this one?

He look'd as if it were—so sought to learn

If punishment, self-order'd, could avail

To oust the devils from the heart of man.

"It is, your grace, of sovereign excellence,"

Replied the abbot, he of Malmesbury,

Pleased with the matter, and the power to speak,

"It draws the venom from the poison'd soul

England," enumerates several of the royal and noble refugees who
took shelter at the court of Athelstan, and helped to dissipate or
damp the remorse which, like the vulture of Prometheus, was
evidently gnawing him to death. In developing the theory of his
character, which, as I observed in a former note, I have adopted, I
have taken as favourable a view as possible of his actions and
motives, though poetry, being bound by laws as rigid and imperative
as those of history, must not fly in the face of her sister muse. What
the latter establishes upon evidence, the former is constrained to adopt.

As the leech heels the drug-embitter'd wound.

There's in our abbey, sire, good brother John—

Surnamed the Roarer from his rugged voice—

Somewhat too much inclined to dainty feasts,

And vanities of love-locks, and bright eyes,

Hath scourged himself to virtue ; oft he finds

The lifted lash which he himself applies

Held backwards—doubtless 'tis the old arch-fiend

Who strives to stop the stroke that would expel

The devil subordinate from our brother's flesh.

One morning in his cell—'twas early dark—

He turn'd—a strong and vigorous man he is—

Suddenly swinging his thick lash in front

Where he thought something stood by him.   It fell

On a hard substance, like a leathery hide,

Or ancient parchment.   Then arose a yell

Of pain and anger, and a noise of feet

Pattering in quick retreat.   Stout brother John,

No more impeded, recommenced his work,

And whipp'd as he had never whipp'd before."

Though not entirely could his intellect

Rise o'er the tales of churchmen, Athelstan

Cried somewhat sharply, "But ourselves, ourselves,

What wouldst thou fix for us to undergo ?"

"Your Grace's conscience is too sensitive,"

Replied the abbot.   "'Twas the will of Heav'n

That the Prince drown'd himself, and left the boat,

Now free to work its disencumber'd way

And land in Kent his innocent follower"—

Then, as he saw his speech pleased not the king,

"I speak the thing your Grace commands to speak ;

And I suggest that for a year, your Grace

Abstain from wine, and from the richer foods,

That please the palate, and the joys of sense,

That are allowed to kings, as to the men

Whom they rule over.   Such a simple life

Will leave the mind and body of my lord

Unweaken'd, to bear up, as is his wont,

The pillars of the land he loves so much."

Then Athelstan, "This were a vanity

Done for the praise of men ; to deprecate

God's wrath, why should we in the creature's sight

Parade a penance ?   Nay, that fated boat

That, bearing Edwin from us, bore away

Our peace of mind, this will we have fetch'd here,

And cut sharp wedges from its wooden ribs,

And strew therewith our nightly couch, whereon

We'll lie in secret sufferance, wearing out

Our seven years' penance, and the wrath of Heav'n."

At this the Abbot, whose well-balanced mind

Saw a right act more righteous in a king,

Broke out amazed at such excess of zeal,

And smoothly talk'd—although he deem'd it true—

Of surplusage of merit, which his Grace

Would store his conscience with, and draw thereon

When the necessities of future sins

Might urge their claim, discounting punishment

For ready payment.   Yet he could not choose

But tell another tale of brother John,

And how he sat too long one wicked night

In sensual revelry, and drank and sang,

Miscalculating the particular sum

Of merit, bought by penance ; thus he spent

His stock of virtue faster than the wine.

So, at the instant when the balance turn'd

Against him, the foul fiend was heard to laugh

And strike him such a buffet on the cheek,

That he fell senseless down, and there was found

Hours after, when men came to clear the room,

With a disorder'd dress, and brain that ached

Sharply, e'en yet, from that Satanic blow.

But seeing that the King spake not, and look'd

As if he heard not, the good priest thought fit

To cease from talking too, and next day left

For Malmesbury, endow'd with further gifts,

And therefore with more power of serving Heav'n.

Still restless thoughts held empire o'er the breast

Of him who claim'd o'er more than half the isle
Unwavering rule ; and with unquiet zeal
He struck out in the busy sea of life
For glory, and his country's furtherance.

    Men oft decide upon their acts, and then
Deliberate on the action that is best.
So was the Council set at Buckingham.
In his most kingly robes there sat the king ;
His silken cloak was rich with flowers that sprang
In form like nature's, but which art had grown
Of golden substance.   Richly gilt his shoes
And tied with purple thongs, conceal'd the foot
High as the ankle, with an opening cleft
Along the instep's rise ; and from his side
In golden scabbard hung his dreadful sword.
He held a sceptre on whose jewell'd top
A dove appear'd to flutter with soft wings ;
And this did he stretch forth, indicative
Of mercy, when the court was merciful.

A second sword lay near, huge, double-edged,

Which, lifted from its rest, appall'd the heart,

And bid hope perish 'ere the word was spoke.

Rich hangings made the walls seem garden-beds,

With singing-birds, and raised embroidery

Of flowers and fruits which wanted taste and smell,

And only those, to perfect the delight.

The blue-ey'd nobles of the land sat round

In their loose-flowing robes of precious silk,

Clasp'd at the breast by gems priced heavily,

With studded belts, and bracelet-girded arms,

And dangling chains, and crested caps, and tunics

That open'd high, and left the neck exposed

To the caresses of the light-hued hair.

Some wore full-lengths of finely-woven hose,

And bandaged cross-wise from the ankle-joint

Unto the knee with party-colour'd strips

Of cloth or leather, blending show with use.

They seem'd like kings, attendants on a king—

A king of warriors, for in many a breast
The heart that throbb'd there beat less joyfully
'Neath peaceful linen than a shirt of mail.
There too the Priests of Christ, of all degrees
Of decorated dignity were met,
From lowest type to metropolitan
(With the pure lamb's-wool pallium round his neck
Bearing upon white ground a bloody cross
Blest by the Papal lips that speak for Heav'n),
To pour the oil of concord, wisely kind,
Over the stormy ocean of debate.

And many things they talk'd of, but the voice
Of Athelstan had such a dominant weight,
That it o'erbalanced every other man's,
Counsellor, earl, or mitred eminence.
Then, mid the rest, a charge was brought to bear
Against a Saxon noble, rich and strong,
But not so rich he was as not to covet
Another's goods, and strong enough to take.

So on the highways he would sally forth,

And when less warlike travellers offer'd him

Their worldly goods in payment for their lives,

He closed the bargain with a courteous haste.

The present victim to his lawless taste,

Was a thin pilgrim from the holy East ;

His cargo that was visible uppermost

Was flakes of wiry hair, and yellow teeth,

And such-like relics of dead saints, that drew

The golden gain of Christian worshippers

To shrines which had no other sanctity.

The noble plunderer cast these relics out

With a profane toss of his weighty hand,

As worthless of regard, and then he found

Bottom'd upon the chest rich smuggled silk,

And gems, and such things which lay easily

In their soft bedding, and in little round

Wrapt up much value—these reposing lurk'd

Under the cover and the countenance

Of those blest remnants of mortality.
Calm then, tho' stern, the voice of Athelstan
As he gave sentence forth, that he who broke
The laws of England, was not fit to share
The honour of their making.   The high court,
Where the king sat as Head, must not be soil'd
By least impurity of membership,
Whoe'er the offender be, whate'er his blood
Peer of the church, or rooted royally.

Pity it was, in that old Parliament
Some great men sat whose faith and practices
Liked not the monarch's notions ; but they smiled
And fear compelled th' assent which love denied.

Then the king spoke of Eldred and his voice
Grew somewhat weaker, as he told how death
Was dealt upon that false conspirator.
And he said, " Hastily my anger sent
This man to his account.   It was the heat

Of hatred for my brother's murderer,

Which made me burn to antedate the voice

Of this great meeting, that would doubtless lie

In the direction where my act hath run,

But whose ask'd sanction should of right precede

The violence that takes a noble's life."

Here the brave Thanes assented with their hearts ;

Edwin was loved, and somebody was kill'd

For having kill'd him—'twas enough, at least,

One victim for the present, and they clash'd

Their arms together for a warrior's vote.

Then the king added, " Hear our further thought !

Of this man's goods we would allot enough

To buy what Nature asks for in the wife

And the young children which he left behind.

But for the rest, it would demean the state

To fatten on the price of traitorous blood—

The blood of him who slew her well-beloved.

'Twere better for his soul that it should pass

To holy use ; that God's interpreters

May crave God's pardon for the man who met

None from his fellow-men.   And so, perchance

The good he does the Church unwittingly

May balance all the voluntary ill

He did when living."   Then did he announce

The names of such known haunts of sanctity

As Ripon, Malmesbury, and Abingdon,

And others.   Thereupon the sacred crowd

Of dignities ecclesiastical,

Knew not which most to praise, the charity

Or wisdom of the king.   His counselling Thanes

Declared their voice that thus the funds should go,

Seeing no chance could give themselves a share.

But the king's eye, which had been overcast

Now rose and sparkled, as it fell on Wales

And Cumberland and Scotland, who had sent

Their Princes delegate and subordinate,

To meet the English king at Buckingham.

Then did he speak to them in thoughtful haste,

Casting forth blame, as willing to provoke

The conduct that he blamed ; and Wales rejoined

In forced humility, that he had paid

Tribute or service, or whate'er was due,

Without declining from the bond one breadth

Of distance the most small, which might offend

The microscopic eye of Majesty.

" Nay ! but ye have not placed," cried Athelstan,

" Your hands in mine, ye tributary lords !

And signified your mere dependency."

" We are prepared to do it "—but they stopt,

Check'd in the full confession of their speech.

For partly in premeditated wrath

Answer'd the king, and partly led away

By the occasion and the words, to feel

The anger that he feign'd, " It is an insult

To wait the ordering what is paid unask'd

By all who know their debts.   When sovereigns claim

Compliance with their will, 'tis not enough

That men should bend and bow, and not gainsay

A thing they cannot thwart—'tis not the act

Suffices as the manner of its doing,

To fill up the full round of reverence.

With scorpions will I whip you, ye proud chiefs !

Until ye show a front that better fits

The height of my position, and your own !" *

Then Wales and Cumberland grew red with rage,

And the words stammer'd on their lips, prepared

For fierce rejoinder ; but the Scottish Prince

With smiling speech whose outward show belied

The soul within it cried, " Be calm, good friends !

King Athelstan can play the game of words

Better than we.   But should the life be beaten

From the bruis'd body on the battle-field,

Words will be useless then to brave or save.

* The records of the grudging chroniclers scarcely yield sufficient
light to guide us through the labyrinth of Athelstan's reign, which,
accordingly, is as full of obscurity as it is of glory.   All the Saxon
princes, when amusement or occupation ran low, sought diligently
for pretexts of quarrels with their neighbours, so that Athelstan at
Buckingham, by giving offence to the Princes of Wales, Scotland,
and Cumberland only followed the example of his predecessors.

We'll try the chance ! "   And the three started up,

Defiance in their looks, and in their feet

And in their hearts a haste which grudged all time

Thrust in 'twixt them and vengeance.   Athelstan

Felt the large spirit throbbing in his breast,

While glory like a glittering siren rose

Before his eyes, and sang to him, and said,

" Great is thy country—make it greater still !

Bright is thy fame—but brighter yet remains ! "

And the king saw no other sight than this,

And he could think no other thoughts than these.

BOOK IV.

Again at York was Athelstan the king,

For, wisely active, he from place to place

Transferr'd his ruling presence.   Foes must fear,

And friends be made to trust ; much care it takes

To keep in hand an empire won by arms.

Yet often was the royal soul diffused

With a large joy that shut out other thoughts,

As in the banquet-hall he sat, and look'd

Upon his brother-soldiers, iron men,

Who loved him with the joy which warriors feel

For those who lead them to destroy the foes

Which hatred makes, or glory simulates.

They, thus content till they again should fight,

Sat long, and drank to victories past, and fed

With what had been the wish that long'd for more.

And, 'mong the rest, amid their wine they talk'd—

Wine pure and strong, or hotly mix'd with spice

And honey-sweeten'd—of the glorious days

When the torn hosts of Wales and Cumberland

Were scatter'd in the battle, as the wind

Scatters the spray-drops of the boastful waves ;

And the proud King of Scotland, Constantine,

Promising fealty, put his son in pawn.

For far Dunfreda saw the English troops

Stand at her walls, nor felt her battlements

Secure against their multitudinous rush ;

And the arm'd ships of Athelstan the Great

Swept through the waves, and show'd like warlike

    ghosts

Before the startled burghers of Caithness.

  At other times the soul of Athelstan

Was vext with thought, the thought that hath not fear,

But which would hold the future in its grasp,

Yet cannot take in the whole round of it.

For well he knew that Anlaf of the Seas

'Twixt Scandinavia and the Irish coast

Would make a pathway, ever stirring up

The elemental hate of neighbourhood,

The love of justice, and the love of prey.

His Irish principality being small

For his outgrown ambition, he would long

To seize the staff his Danish father bore,

And, beating down the heads of opposition,

Extend it o'er the men and realms of Wessex.

So from the settlements which struck their roots

In Ireland's soil, and from the Baltic shores,

Would rise a cry to curse the Saxon king,

And swell the hopes of Anlaf with its breath.

Bright was the day that saw the princely Dane

Embark from Ireland's hospitable coast

For Scandinavia's realm, where Death had set

A workshop up to forge the bolts of war ;

And brighter far his hopes than when he sought
Those shores at first, the fugitive of fight,
And only not defeated in the soul
That cast misfortune from it, as the shield
Of a great chief repels the petulant darts
Hurl'd at him by some minor combatants.
Long troops of friends went with him to the shore,
Fierce friends, who prized his warlike aptitudes,
And gentler ones, who loved the face and form
Of the young prince, nor less for dangers past,
And the ambitious future's prominence.

And when the ship plunged boldly on the essay
Of its long travel on that ocean-road,
From level sands, and rocky points, and heights
Of humble roofs, and rough-raised battlements,
Came shouts and wavings and the clash of arms,
Like signals sent from wishing hearts that blest
That vessel's dealings with the faithless sea.
And proudly she, that early ship, went forth,

As feeling how upon her back she bore
The heir of a great fate.   Slow sank the land
Behind the green convexity, and then
Each noise came fainter on the favouring wind,
And noble pennants look'd like tiny rags
Scarce seen in th'azure distance of the air.

   Away, away ; and nothing now around
But the blue stretch of waters ; and for cheers
Were ordering voices and responsive cries,
And creaking ropes, and the upheaving wash
Of parted waves—and Anlaf turned to think
Upon the friends he could no longer see.
Then, when the sun was low—a golden brooch,
Joining the earth and sky—he watch'd it set
Royally mid a retinue of clouds
And the bright service of reflected light,
As subjects shine when monarchs smile on them.
Long rippled belts of sky were beautiful
With tints of saffron and of amethyst

Made brilliant by a surface-film of gold.

While higher up etherial cloudlets perched,

Hover'd like fleecy flames in the grey air.

Then faint and fainter every glory grew,

And a thin darkness settling o'er the scene,

He listen'd to the waves, as if he long'd

To find a voice in their monotonous plash

To tell him of his fate.   At last the moon

Rose up behind her watery parapet,

And look'd upon the ocean.   Lines of fire

Stream'd forth from her full-bodied orb, and made

A shining pathway o'er the tremulous sea,

A road of scintillating silver, fit

For the green-vested fairies of the deep.

   The happy spirit of the scene suffused

The breast of Anlaf, as he calmly read

The glowing sight as a good prophecy.

And with the night he dreamt of kingdoms won

Too easily for fame, and how he liv'd

To rule o'er subjects loving to be ruled.

And all the next day through the southern winds

Seem'd leagued with Anlaf's hopes to speed his way—

The way to Fortune, never reach'd too soon.

On the third early morning, as the sun

Just lit the white tops of the dancing waves,

A ship was seen that had an evil look

In the left distance.   They of Anlaf's crew

Fear'd as they view'd it bearing down on them

With a sharp haste that had a threat of harm.

Nearer it came, and then too visible

Its nature was to the desponding eyes

Of those who felt they had no strength to match

Its lawless prowess—yet the fear was less

Of dying, than of being forced to die

With but slight chance of giving death for death.

Thus did they see that ship, a floating curse,

Rapine and slaughter-freighted, prompt to turn

Where'er its pirate-lord, the Viking, will'd

To launch it at some ocean-traveller.

Nearer it came, and running rapidly,

Like a fierce serpent with a hundred feet.

Long was its shape, and sharp, and curvingly

It rose with poop-deck and with forecastle

Above the waters; a gilt dragon's head

Shone horribly in front, and at the end

Its tail curl'd upwards, fold on deadly fold,

Over the helmsman's head.   From stem to stern

The rails were hung with shields of white and red,

Looking like scales upon the monstrous back

Of some sea-animal.   On each side its legs

Were never still, as double banks of oars

Plied their quick lengths to aid the bellying sails.

Defence was idle—'twere as well for one,

A naked-handed man, to brave the snake

That in an Indian wood, with mighty grip,

Wraps itself round the tiger, king of beasts,

And from the crack'd ribs squeezes out the life.

What could Prince Anlaf do ?   Thought fail'd him then.

'Twere base to yield, and yet 'twas hard to die,

To perish thus, before his hand could grasp

The fruit which he had cultur'd with such care.

Thought fail'd him then, and so it seem'd to him

That his eyes fail'd him too, for on the deck

Of the strange ship now closing on its prey

He saw a man, prepar'd to head th' attack ;

A short strong man, below himself in age

One year or more—'twas Guthforth—and the two

Soon used for brotherly regard the hands

With which each thought to snatch the other's life

Or to protect his own.   Then Guthforth cried,

"Come in good time, my brother !   I can now

Convoy thee where thou wilt, and save thy friends

From such unmannerly rovers as myself."

So Anlaf mounted on his brother's ship,

Hailing the chance that blew his fears away.

And left his scheme of empire yet unnipt.

And the two brothers, as the ship sped on

To its far haven, talk'd of many things—
Of the much-varied past, and if the future
Would in good faith redeem the promises
Made for it by the present.   But to all
That Anlaf urged to work on Guthforth's love,
And lead him to cast in his lot with his,
The other answer'd, "Brother mine, enough !
Whene'er you wish to cross the seas I have
A good steed at your service : as for land,
I've tried it, and I hate it.   Both I've tried,
Scot, Saxon—Athelstan and Constantine.
The former is the better—gives good wine,
And plenty—try it, when you mount the throne !
But the Scot keeps a beggarly table—ah !
Would he were here ! I'd show my gratitude,
And feed him on salt-water."   Anlaf cried,
" Be serious, brother !   'Tis an earnest thing
That we discourse of."   "Serious !" he replied,
"Serious it is to be shut up a month
And fed on cursed concoctions,—things like fat

Stew'd up with entrails! And for drink—great Odin!

Would he were here! And what, good Anlaf, say

Would the land give me that the sea denies?

Here on my golden dragon do I sit,

Unquestion'd monarch of a widening realm,

Unbounded as we stand, and boundless still

With the advances of a thousand miles.

'Twould be a bold hand his, who'd draw the teeth

Of my salt-serpent. *Should* I meet a foe

To check the gallop of my ocean-stag,

My courser o'er the causeway of the deep,

The strong arm settles our supremacy—

Good honest blows—and not the drivelling skill

Of cravens, which men call diplomacy.

Gods! how I hate that devil's ability

That passes lies, like bastards, upon Truth

As their sworn father, who knows naught of them.

Why—half my crew could do the thing as well,

If they could stomach its sheer dirtiness!

And then, for health!—We need not talk of that:

Feel how the gale streams on our faces, pure

As when it started first to sweep the sea,

Untouch'd by man, who what he touches taints.

Thou seekest power. I *have* it. *This* is power,—

To take the storm that whistles in my face,

As it would blow my life out in its scorn,

And bind it down in chains of art, a slave,

To drag me o'er the waves that heave in vain

To overset my elemental throne.

My willing subjects love and fear me both,

And fear, too, begets love, for they can see,

Being wise in their own line, that this without,

I could not slip them in well-order'd bands,

To reap the golden crops that please them most."

"Nay!" Anlaf said, "how eloquent this air

Hath made you! Love that talks of what it loves,

Of what it loves talks well. Didst thou e'er speak

To Edwin of this governable sea?"

And Guthforth answer'd not, but o'er his face

There pass'd a thought of anger and of grief;

But, changing mood, he cried, " Come brother Anlaf,

My consort and my queen will sing the sea

And its delights, to cast my prose in shade.

I'll fetch her.   When she fled away with me

From Scotland, by the gods ! I think we left

Nothing worth staying for behind,—in fact

'Tis a bleak country ; and their food—" "The song !"

Cried Anlaf, hastily, "The song !"   And soon

The lady stept on deck ; a girl-like face

But pretty, with short figure, scarcely slim.

Her auburn tresses rivall'd in their hue

The health of her round cheek.   Her look was fraught

With quiet sense, but which her eye declared

Could flash with passion of more kinds than one.

The water and the winds accompanied

With loving cadence her unprest-for song.

O, Love ! it is like the sea,
    Which rolls as it e'er hath roll'd,

K

So fresh in its life, so free,
  And never tired out, nor old!
    To me, to me,
      Love seems to be like the sea!

Behold, how to it 'tis giv'n
  To mix with the skies above!
The sea hath the love of Heav'n,
  And hearts have the heav'n of love.
    To me, to me,
      Love seems to be like the sea!

Tho' the sea be deep, not more
  'Tis so than a love that's true,
And only when near the shore
  Doth the ocean change its hue.
    To me, to me,
      Love seems to be like the sea!

For the brave 'tis good to sit
  On the steed of the stormy wave;
So ever is Love most fit
  For the joy of the good and brave.
    To me, to me,
      Love seems to be like the sea!

O ! how when the Tempest breaks,
  The sea into wild life starts !
So the spirit of Love awakes
  The passion of human hearts.
        Yes, yes, to me,
    Love ever is like the sea !

"A charming song !" quoth Anlaf; "yet I trust
Love is *not* like the sea, which wanders much,
And hugs a hundred shores in its embrace."
Here Guthforth smiled, and shook his head ; but she,
The sovereign of his heart, both smiled and frown'd.

  And so the brothers talk'd from day to day,
Quaffing sea-air, 'till Scandinavia's coast
Rose like a darkness on the northern wave :
Then, as more near the golden dragon crept,
The cloud resolved itself in form of land—
Round rocky hills, upon whose sides the pine
Made the dark thickness of a tangled wood
Going down to meet the shore, where blocks detach'd

From mountain-masses lay in sullen strength,

Wounding the ground in their indignant fall.

Close by the coasts low stony islets ran,

Set there like outworks to resist th' attack

Of the loud-surging armies of the deep.

'Twixt main and islands, interthreading rocks

And topping stone-mounds, flow'd th' impetuous sea.

Thus, land and waters look'd as shaken up

By the world's Maker, and then cast abroad

To settle down in chance companionship

And intermixture of their elements.

Near where a heap of jagged rock shot up

From a smooth rounded base, an index-mark

To point the passage, Guthforth sought the shore,

Follow'd by Anlaf; then they wound their way

Into the wild recesses of the land.

A rugged way it was; a narrow cleft

'Twixt lofty cliffs that rose on either hand

Like adamantine walls to the bleak sky.

Over their summits ice-cold torrents fell,

And, plunging down from shelf to rocky shelf,

Were dash'd thereby into a watery dust.

Below, a rapid stream rush'd quarrelling

With stocks and stones that loiter'd in its path

Like idlers in a flood of working men ;

While birch and alder, richly arch'd o'erhead

In noisy canopies, sway'd to and fro

Before the gusty onsets of the wind.

At length the two were met by messengers

Who knew of Anlaf's coming, and by these

The royal pair were welcomed royally

And made a Danish noble's well-fed guests.

There too they rested, each on skin-clad couch,

And dreamt, the one of captures made at sea,

The other of an empire won on land. *

---

* History is sparing of its revelations respecting the heroic Northumbrian Anlaf, who made the crown totter on the head of Athelstan, and perhaps was only prevented by accident from placing it
on worthier brows. It was his misfortune that he aimed at victory
through the swords of the Danes, who had grown to be so hated in

And after busy days, the war-horns woke

The country round, and unto every spot

Where knots of men, in rude companionship,

Were cluster'd into dwellings, arrows split

Into four parts, were sent, as summoning

A full assembly to be held in arms.

Strange were the counsellors that gather'd there

To that fierce parliament, and less th' intent

In long debate to moot the right of war,

Than hear, in fiery phraseology,

Excuse for doing what they long'd to do.

Tall, wiry, handsome-featured, somewhat slight,

The warrior-nobles sat or stood in bands,

Conversing in quick speech, and strengthening

Their arguments with action, most like blows

Struck at a foeman ; nor were wanting there

England for their multiplied atrocities, that justice itself would
have been detested if upheld by them. Yet it seems probable that
Anlaf had no other choice, since his Irish and Scotch allies, though
brave, were insufficient in numbers to encounter the force of England
under Athelstan.

Men of more low degree, all lesser ranks
Who could wear arms, and understood their use.

   'Twas a large plain, if plain it might be call'd,
That was not mountainous, but merely ridged
By rough projecting mounds, or lengthwise seam'd
By stony hollows.   Ancient trees grew there,
Dumb witnesses of unremember'd deeds.
And stretch'd from branch to branch, or pole to pole,
Sail-canvass form'd an awning ; never yet
Were heads so countless cover'd by a roof.
And Anlaf stood upon a rise, and look'd
With throbbing heart on his compatriots, ranged
Before his eyes, a very sea of men,
Now still, in living undulations mass'd.
And lifting up his right hand, thus he spake.

   " Ye are my countrymen, and therefore brave,
True Danes ye are, and surely therefore just.
And whensoever Justice sees the right,

It rests with Valour to redress the wrong.

What *are* my rights?   Is there a father here

Whose son hath been despoil'd by violence?

Is there a son amongst you whose sire died

A death that brave men die not willingly?

Then can they feel why I, unskill'd to scatter

The flowers of speech, hold up the naked truth

As the broad banner for our gathering.

Brave countrymen, how rich is England!   Yet

I would not urge you on that bad pretence,

Not e'en to conquer back the Danish wealth

Sack'd by the Saxon soldiery at York.

But follow me 'gainst him who made himself

A king by killing,—a most cruel brother,—

Who wash'd his hands in nearest kinsmen's blood,

And cried, 'Now am I pure to govern well,

Having slain all who would have govern'd worse.'

Cursed logic!   Where is Ælfred?—Ethelwald?

Where Edwin?   Ask the poison and the knife,

And the impervious prison of the sea.

Usurper !   Faithless friend ! and bastard son !

Why, friends, how many names hath Athelstan

To cause your passion rise, and deal on him

A separate death for separate infamies ?

'Tis not a common thing for Denmark's sons

To let their kingdoms suffer hard assault,

Thieves take their riches off, and tyrants send

Their princes to unprincely banishment,—

And shall it be so now ?   Let him who likes

Commence the custom !   Hear me, countrymen !

I swear by yon round candle of the gods

That lights up their empyreal palaces,

I do not call you to this bath of blood,

To raise the smoke of horse-hoofs from the soil,

To bid your bow-strings loose the birds of war,

On the mere hope to reap the crop of spoil

In an unjust contention ; but when right

Hallows the march of Danish armaments,

Then will I speak of England's wondrous wealth,

Her own self-got, and what her hands have robb'd

From others, Scotland, Wales, and Cumberland,

And your own unforgotten countrymen !

Behold the ample prey, whose choicest part,

If each man had ten hands, would baffle him

To hold it, after he has dropt the sword

Red with the day's long work, and well content

E'en if it won no other prize than that

More rich than all, the life-blood of a foe !"

Low murmuring cries, as Anlaf spake, kept growing

Like the far mutters of advancing clouds

Instinct with lightning, bursting, when he ceased,

Into a roar of voices, never heard

But when hearts flash with feeling, and the lips

Follow in thunder of articulate sounds.

Chiefs, upon oval shields rang out their joy,

Dashing their lance-heads on them, or held high

To Heav'n their war-anticipating swords.

And at the instant the clear sun shone out

On opposite rain-clouds, turning their round drops

To colour'd crystals, and a mighty arch
Sprang like a bridge of triple hues from earth
To make a roadway for immortal hopes.

And Anlaf trembled with delight to think
That from this prosperous sowing of the soil
Would spring the harvest of a great success.
So on from hour to hour, and day to day,
Active he strove and thought ; and passing back
To Ireland, stirr'd the flame there, fanning it
With argument of honour, and the love
Of mere excitement, and the hope of prey.
Then once again to Scandinavian land,
That bred his kith and kin, to organise
The elements of aid, and shape and strengthen
Th' ideas, and loves, and hatreds, upon which
He based the unknown future of his hope.
Next, soon as order grew, and men and arms
Roll'd to the sea-coast, where the ships lay tied
Like beasts of burden, ready pack'd to bear

His fierce supporters, slowly from the mist
That ever hides what yet remains undone,
The throne of Wessex seem'd to shine, like light
Diffused in cloudy splendour through a fog.

And when at sea, how Anlaf tried in joy
To count the ships that seem'd as numberless
As were the waves on which they rose and fell.
Upon each deck a part of all the hopes
On which he lived was carried to the goal.
And, day by day, from out th' uncertain line
Of the horizon, topmasts rear'd their heads
Adorn'd with pennants, slowly, till the hulls
Roll'd up like bodies of huge ocean-beasts
Leaving their dens for breath of fresher air.
Each one with sails display'd, and flashing oars,
Converged its course upon the central fleet,
Helping to swell those savage elements
Of war and rapine. So may torrents dash'd
From rocky heights seek some great river's mouth

To fill its foaming jaws, till they disgorge
In the deep sea their stormy aggregate.

   Nor then was Ireland wanting in her love
And hate, for Anlaf, and for Athelstan.
Some fifty vessels sallied from her ports
With such a crowd of boisterous combatants,
One might have fear'd they left themselves no noise
To greet the gaining of a victory.
And as the fleet drew near the English coast,
They saw long lines of dust, and, borne by winds,
Heard distant thunders of tumultuous men
As if in motion—'Twas the gather'd force
Of Wales and Cumberland and Scotland, pour'd
Along the shore-way to that mighty flood
Of war to add its tributary stream.
And Anlaf felt and look'd, and look'd and felt,
And every sight and every thought inflamed
His spirit till it glow'd.   His right hand stretch'd,
As if in vision, shook in air—not more

It would have trembled had it held a crown.

From time to time, borne chance-ways from the sea,
There came these tidings unto Athelstan
Of how the wave grew larger, night by night,
To overwhelm his empire, and to leave
Himself a wreck upon the wasted shore.
Therefore the wary leader held at York
The council and the feast, and gather'd force
To mate with force, and strengthen'd all defence
To break the onfall of the barbarous tide.

Naught for a foe of earth cared Athelstan ;
And as he raised the bowl up to his lips
To drink confusion to the Danish dogs,
There came in one who brought an arrow, wrapt
With a thin strip of paper—shot, he said,
Into the camp, and found there, plunging deep
Its iron shod beneath the soil, and bound
Beneath the feathers with what seem'd to him

A written letter; but he could not read,

Though he could fight, and boast of noble blood.

Then the king took the paper, on whose back

Was writ, "To the usurper Athelstan!"

Within, short phrase, but meaning many things—

"My right to England's throne is Edwin's death."

"Again!" cried Athelstan, and o'er his face

There pass'd, soon vanishing, the look of him

Who fears lest he be thought to fear, and next

Wrath with himself for having worn that look.

Then, crumpling up the paper he exclaim'd,

"He must be here, and near—search!—Nay, no matter!

'Twould take a hundred princes of his breed

To shake the popular throne of Athelstan!

Fool! doth he think that 'tis for him or his

These Danish hell-hounds whet the teeth of war?"

Next falling thoughtful, "Would he were alive!"

He said, and sigh'd in short sincerity.

"Why ever thus?—a useless obstacle

In the mid-stream of action!—Died he not

By his own act?"   And as his voice grew louder

Uttering the last words, some one near him cried—

It boots not who ; a king knows many such—

" Your grace says true ; he died"—But Athelstan

Spake sharply, shamed of having shown his shame,

" Who ask'd thee for thy speech?"; and then there

      came

A second messenger, who told how ships

Descried from heights upon the eastern coasts

Blacken'd the distant waves, more numerous

Than ever yet, since Scandinavia sent

Her first-born hordes to settle where they liked

And plunder where they pleased.   No trace of thought

Struggling to hide its bitterness now blurr'd

The open mirror of the royal face,

Whence was reflected to examining eyes

The boldness that turns danger to a joy.

Short answer made the king.   " Thus will we break

The power of Denmark," and he snapt in twain

The arrow which he held, and brake again

Each bit into two other bits, and cast

The fragments from him with a passionate scorn.

    The broad-mouth'd Humber* rolls its waves, full-fed

By friendly waters, tributes from the lands

That bend around, and stretching like the boughs

Of some huge tree (more great than those that grew

When men were giants) which has fallen to earth,

And bare of leaves the agèd ruin lies.

So doth it roll till Saltfleet and Spurnhead,

Like watchmen on their towers, behold it pass

Into the life of Ocean and there die.

* The Humber may justly be regarded as among the most historical of England's streams, since it was into its broad mouth that all the buccaneering rascaldom of the North poured their fury and thirst of plunder, down to the day in which the sons of Sweyn, contemporary with Harold, the son of Godwin, brought doubtful and treacherous aid to the patriots cooped up in the fens. Yet our national geographers have scarcely been at sufficient pains to explore and point out the spots on which our ancestors bled to preserve the independence of their country. Thrasymene and Allia, the Granicus, Cunaxa and Gaugamela, have employed and exhausted the learning of a hundred antiquarians; while Fulford-gate, Stamford on the Derwent, and Brunnaburgh, are enveloped in almost mythical obscurity. A volume of profound interest might still be written on the topography of the Humber and its tributaries.

The sun was sinking low, beset by clouds

Fastening upon the brightness of his beams,

Which struggled through them, shooting whitely up

Like rays from a colossal coronet.

Part of the scene was cast in shade by hills,

But through the open, the high-tided waters

Shone with small light from the descending globe ;

And brokenly they shone, as through them plunged

The cruel keels of twelve times fifty ships,

The vehicles of an invading hate.

Such were the floating thrones, that, wheel'd on waves

And drawn in triumph by the storm-winds, bore

The sovereigns of the sea—not gentle kings,

With gorgeous robes, in lamp-lit palaces,

But clad in strong coarse garments, to repel

The tempest and the battle ; treading floors

That heaved as heaves the many-headed deep.

While the high roof above them sometimes shone

Spotted with mild magnificence of stars,

Sometimes with lightning seam'd, whose jagged glare

Could blind the eyes that never wink'd at death.

The thunder was their music as it peal'd,

Or clash of hostile arms; or softer sound

Of money chinking on the deck, and dropt

In thankfulness for being allow'd to live.

For Dane and Norseman now, with Ireland's chiefs

And Scot and Kymrian leagued, have sworn an oath

Upon their golden bracelets to avenge

The death of Sihtric upon Athelstan;

And to reseat the son where erst the sire

Sat royally, and to prolong that seat

(If force and numbers do their wonted work)

Unto the Saxon's native empiry.

The blast that drove the war-ships, symbolised

The stormy ruin brooding o'er the land.

Upon each vessel's prow, a lion's head

Grinn'd horribly, or a fierce dragon there

Spread its unnatural and insulting wings;

While bulls and monsters of the sea display'd,

In clumsy yet repulsive portraiture,

The people's pow'r to do the thing they loved,

For they loved fighting, and they fought too well.

Birds on the creaking top-masts seem'd to hover

In flight for England, and with outstretch'd beaks

Clamour for food.   To many a ship were hung,

High round its sides, the batter'd shields that yet

Had not unlearnt their work, and could confront

The battle and the blow.   Near, nearer came

Those dreadful hulls—and warriors sprang to land,

Which did recoil from the unmannerly tread

That lighted on its breast.   Each savage chief

Who found his feet sink in the loamy earth,

Dug his stout javelin in its depths to stay

His goings o'er the soil he call'd his own.

His thirsty followers pour'd like countless troops

Of wild dogs, pitiless and infuriate,

With hard gaunt bodies, patient to endure,

And whose keen spirits scent the distant blood.

Soon was the whole land strew'd confusedly
With bow and battle-axe and two-edged sword,
Nail-studded club, and sling, and iron shield,
And men scarce softer than the arms they bore.

Nor did the Saxon king forget his trust,
Now, in the empire's peril, and he sent
A chosen army to dispel the clouds
Of this invasion, and to crush the hordes
Whose life was battle, and whose love was spoil.
There on the Deira's edge, and on the front
Of Northern Mercia they encamp'd, and stood
Rock-like, and offering their firm breasts to bar
The incursive tide, whose fast-approaching roar
Was as the shout of warriors ere they strike.

And many were the foes of Athelstan
Who raised their heads and hopes up, crying out
" Now is the hour for crime to pay the price
At which it bought success." And ev'n his friends

Found now the soil of danger breed a crop

Of fears and doubts, and thoughts ne'er thought before

O'ercloud the noon of their opinion.

But neither friend nor enemy dared speak

A doubt or fear in presence of the king;

And e'en their looks grew brighter as they gazed

On the untroubled spirit in his face,

That lit it, as the sun some fortress-tow'r

That stands before th' assaulting catapult,

And, careless of the stones and fiery darts

Flung at it, looks from its superior crown

In quiet strength upon the brawling foe.

BOOK V.

Not far from York there spread a patch of ground
Sloping on all sides slightly to a depth
Not greater than a warrior helmeted
Would measure from his crest.   The soil below
Was circular in shape, and soft and green,
And through it, with scarce sensible wave, there flow'd
A streamlet, cool and silent as the hour.
It was the hour when healthy labour rests,
And e'en ambition seeks to brace its strength
For larger struggles; when the bad and good
Do good, or evil, only in their dreams.
The hero's arm lay harmless by his side;
They too his victims with to-morrow's light
Were happy in their last repose.   The world

Was sleeping, and its great breast gently heaved
In rise and fall, as if the day ne'er broke
Its peace with care, nor startled it by crime.
Yet in this little spot, dead seemingly
To thought and motion, there was waking life.

'Twas night, not merely by prescriptive right
For lovers' meetings, when the pale moon hears
All the delightful nothings that young hearts
Pour, in their deep unreasoning passion, forth.
Yet were there young hearts here, but secrecy
Was unto them a vital element ;
And the revealing moon, that would have told
Their presence to unfriendly eyes, was hid
Beneath the Earth.   So, by the touch of hands,
And by the sound of voices and of sighs,
And by the instinct of discerning love,
Did the twain know that each was nearest that
Which of all life the other most desired.
" It may not be," said Bertha, " must not be.

Foe unto him, the monarch whom I serve—

Nay, speak not of his faults, or call them crimes—

Stranger to Him, the God whom I adore,

And present here to loose the curse of war

Upon the homes of my ancestral land,

How can I mate with thee ? how fly with thee,

And fly from king, from country, and from Heav'n ?"

" Nay ! Thou mistakest, Bertha !" cried the youth,

" To fly with me is not, I trust my gods,

To fly from king or country, for I hope

To make thy country mine, and raise up thee

To be the Queen which nature made thee for ;

In all things wilt thou gain—the man thou lov'st

Will be the uncrown'd sovereign of thy heart,

And kingly reverence only deepen love :

Thy country will be thine by double right,

For thou shalt rule it, and shalt do it good

In an exact proportion to thy rule.

And for thy God—why keep him, and take mine !

I am content, so thou and they agree."

Then, as he felt the maiden's hand relax

Beneath this lightness—"Bertha! pardon me.

Thou canst not think, knowing me as thou dost,

That, having all thy earthly faith as man,

I could in jealous cruelty forbid

The adoration of an unseen God!"

"But to live bound," said Bertha, "live *so* bound;

Be one with one whose creed is not my creed.

To feel that part as 'twere of my own self

Will co-exist with me but some few years,

And then be sever'd for all ages, far

As is thy Heav'n from mine!" "Again reflect,"

Rejoin'd her lover with severer voice,

"There is a passage somewhere in the book

Thou holdest as the Volume of the World,

Which says the erring husband may be caught

And chain'd to Wisdom like a rock, by her

Who loves like him, but thinks more holily."

She answer'd not, but to the darkness sigh'd

So strangely, and with meaning that convey'd

The love of man, and love of God, and doubt

Of her own pow'r for good, with shy distrust

Of woman's arguments ; and then the thought

Of serving Heav'n came uppermost, as if

Deep at the root no human passion lay.

But, starting from her trance, she rapidly

Exclaim'd, " Yet hear !   'Tis said thou hast for wife

A daughter of the Scottish Constantine.

A Christian woman may not part her love,

And give a heart in half for half a heart !"

" Bertha !" he answer'd—" Bertha ! trust me here.

When men stretch out their unassisted hands

To pull a king from off his throne, and seat

Themselves thereon, 'twill fall upon and crush

Th' invaders into dust ; and so they need

A lift from foreign aid.   Honour alike

And prudence bind me to conceal the bond

I made with Scotland—Bertha ! trust me here.

I swear by—nay, thou wilt not trust my gods.

By thy own true divinity I swear

I will not wed thee, will not pray thee wed me,

Unless I be as pure from earthly tie

As is the whitest angel in thy Heav'n.

Dost thou believe me?"   "Freely," answer'd she,

" I *do* believe thee, else I could not love.

There is no falsehood in thy heart, so none

Can issue to thy tongue; but—but!"—and then

The youth grew passionate in his plea, as seeing

That time was short, and that in that short time

Lay all his hope of her who unto him

Was as the kingdom of Northumbria—

"Love! trust! what would'st thou more? a name which
          deeds

Will illustrate yet beyond the rank I drew

From my own father's royal marriage-bed?

And what opposes?—thy allegiance

To a usurping murderer's bastardy!

Thy country, faith, friends—keep them all, and gain

Myself beside, thy subject and thy king!

O, Bertha! who am I?   I am not changed

From that bright day—it was not night as now—

When first I met thee in my father's halls.

Thou dost remember when I woo'd thee there,

And from thy silence and thy trembling drew

A happy omen, more than from thy words.

I did beseech thee but to breathe my name

Familiarly, as one who liked the sound ;

And thou didst fear to do it, I being by,

But pledged thy promise to me, when I went,

To send it after my departing steps.

Then, with thy head aside, in half-heard tones,

As I retreated, thou didst whisper 'Anlaf !'

And further off, as slowly, slowly going,

I heard ' dear Anlaf !', round the senseless air

That bore such words, I threw my arms to kiss

The impalpable sweetness of that atmosphere !

Come with me, Bertha !   Come, and grow more bold,

And grow more happy too."   But Bertha spake not.

The hand of night conceal'd the thoughts that past

Across her face in short convulsive change.

But there was heard the trembling of her limbs,

Shaking her garments, from the head-rail clasp'd

Round neck and shoulder, fold o'er silken fold,

Down to the nether kirtle at her feet.

And then there came a low small resolute voice,

As one might breathe who hath made up his mind

To leave a home which he delights in, "Anlaf!

My heart is sad—alas! that good intents

Should fail to cheer it!   Reasons I have none.

And yet I feel that in the circumstance

Of place and faith wherein thou art, dear friend,

I cannot go with thee—O, suffer me!

Suffer a woman to pursue the right

In the straight line of sensitive conscience,

Who cannot deviate into proof to show

That what she does is what she ought to do."

Short space she cast herself on him and wept

As if she'd wash her heart into his arms;

Then, with an effort, sprang from him, and fled

Into the still dark solitude secure.

He stood and spake not.　His proud spirit bow'd
Unto the fate he felt had hold on him;
And, with a sigh, he turn'd reluctantly
From the dear spot where she so late had stood,
And follow'd Glory, looking back on Love.

　Long upon Denmark's warlike multitude
The morn had risen, to stir both hands and hearts.
Far from the river had they camp'd, but yet
Sighting their ships, upon a rising ground,
Harder and bare, and broken on its face
By ridges gently sloping from the plain.
In the near distance, amid every pause,
When pause there was of soldiers and their arms,
The wind made moaning in the trees that hung
Upon the backs of the low round-topp'd hills,
As if the voice of nature mourn'd to see
Green England wasted by barbaric tread.

　The sun was venturing on his height of noon;

Round the whole camp a motley wall was raised

Of baggage and of waggons, placed with art

To most encumber an advancing foe.

Beneath huge caldrons on sticks intercross'd,

There crackled waving fires, and water hiss'd

To cook the flesh of horses for the feast.

In other parts swine roasted whole invoked

Applauding comment from the crowds who meant

To draw on glutted appetite for strength

To kill their foemen as they kill'd their food.

Horns of a size commensurate with the thirst

Of strong-limb'd warriors, whose all-day delight

Lay under open skies, in war, and games

That mimick'd best their fierce original,

Leant, ready to be fill'd with wine or ale,

'Gainst stones heap'd up, or dark unleafy bush.

In circles ranged upon the ground they sat

For serious drinking ; as they fought they drank.

A savage grandeur signalised the scene

Of these bold pirates thus enjoying life
Before they took or lost it—better far
For them the latter, than to rest in peace
Beneath the shade of meditative ease,
Or in ill-flavour'd room, to wear away
The dingy days, and rob the nights of sleep
In a monotonous movement of the hands,
Earning scant pittance as the slaves of trade.

But ere the joy of hunger kill'd itself
In eating till Time bid it live again,
Again to die in ceaseless interchange,
They made all ready for a sacrifice
To the great god, from out whose nostril flows
The breath that fans the lurid flame of fight—
That fierce divinity whose welcome draws
The heroes, battle-slain, within the halls
Of his Heaven-founded palace, there to feast
On an unperishing similitude
Of earthly food, and everlasting wine.

M 2

Stones three times seven, the largest sought and
found
Upon that foreign soil, they placed around,
Endwise, and in a mystic circle ranged.
Within this rude and temporary fane
A high-priest led the war-horse; proudly he
Stood with his ears stitch'd up, and nostrils slit,
His training this in battle's bloody school.
A well-directed hatchet-blow let out
The life-blood from his temple, down he sank
On the red ground amid applauding shouts.
Then was the flesh cut up, and boil'd in haste;
And the priest seized the largest piece with tongs
Offering it to his god; next, dipt a brush
In the warm gore yet welling from the wound,
And sprinkled it upon the people round,
A baptism of slaughter, making them
Worthy of Heaven, strong, brave and merciless.
Thereon each chieftain held his weapon high,
And cried "Great Odin! sanctify thy sons.

Strong hands, and fearless hearts, these please thee
          most ;
Make *us* to please thee.   Ancient father ! make
Our hands to strike, our hearts to fear no stroke !"

  A flash of lightning lit the southern sky,
But not a voice of thunder follow'd it.
And from the heaven, which cloudless was and clear,
A few thick rain-drops on the sacrifice
Fell heavily—the omen pleased them not,
And gloomily they stood with arms deprest.

  Then from the ranks stept forth the prophetess,
Helna, tall, young, and fiercely beautiful.
Rolling her wild eye o'er the sullen crowds,
She seem'd to pierce the future, and to link
The present life with it, like fruit and seed.
A silken tunic mystically work'd
With dark blue characters, of strange device,
Upon a yellow ground, begirt her form

Beneath the heaving bosom to the knees.

A kind of robe hung, veil-like, for one side

From the left shoulder, tightly gather'd there

To a small silver arrow, and thence flow'd

Down to the ankle.   Her dismantled locks

Now hid, and now reveal'd her naked breasts

With each impassion'd gesture, as the clouds

Wind-harass'd show and hide th' alternate moon.

A circlet intermix'd of thorns and gold

Bound her high forehead like a diadem.

"Poor measure this," she cried disdainfully,

"Ye give to Odin! this too on the eve

Of a great battle, which should send your names

Yet higher up on valour's catalogue.

The flesh of horses is a common thing

To fill the nostrils of divinity.

On great occasions when ye ask for much,

Ye must give much, and buy your dearest wish

By an exceeding worth of sacrifice.

Hark! to the god now thund'ring from the sky,

And asking human blood—male blood, and young—

Give it him, men ! and prosper—give it not,

Then let fear occupy your cheeks, let fear

Inspire your feet to fly that final shame

When the bold Saxons shall rush forth on you,

And whip you to your ships, like vagrant dogs

That quit their kennels without sufferance ?"

If those rude warriors wanted argument

For such an offering, they could find it there

In flashing eye, and Heaven-appealing arm,

And lip so tremulous with scorn, it seem'd

To warn off love from coming near to it.

"Blood ! human blood !" they shouted ; and then
    chose

Seven candidates—they term'd them so—to stand

On their election to this glorious death.

Among the rest a pretty youth there was,

Scarce sixteen summers on his head had shower'd

Richness of light and colour, and his heart

Beat visibly in his breast, as if it knew

Too little of life's worthlessness as yet

To risk the loss of it contentedly.

He look'd as feeling where the lot would fall,

He look'd as thinking how his mother's shrieks

Would hail the vision of this awful chance—

This terrible lot—and so it fell on him

As he had felt, and then he felt no more.

Closing his eyes he fainted to the earth,

And thence they lifted him, and bore him off

To kill again what seem'd already dead.

Then in the centre of the stone-faced ring,

They raised a broader stone, with rounded top,

To be the bloody altar upon which

To offer up this precious fruit of life,

One seed of murder to secure a crop.

Upon the stone they set the senseless boy ;

Close by him stood the priest—and lifting up

An iron hammer high, three times he pray'd,

Crying "Hear, Odin, and accept !"   A clash

Of beaten arms from all the warriors near,

Gave horrible assent, and woke the child

From his most happy trance.   With large wild eyes

He shriek'd, as seeing all his fate, revived

Only to die again; and round the knees

Of the hard priest he threw his delicate arms—

Embrace the stone, poor fool! and bid it weep.

No answer gave the priest; but raising up

His hand to Heav'n, commenced his second prayer.

Just then a man, with half his armour on,

And hot with travel, spurr'd his panting horse

Through the thick crowds into the centre ring.

'Twas Anlaf—as he motion'd to the priest

To stop that cruel death, his war-steed bent

Its noble head, and snift at the poor boy

Upon the stone, scarce knowing what it was,

That trembling thing, but which his instinct taught

Was made for pity; and thus Anlaf spake.

" Short time, my friends! and then the battle-horn

Will call to fight with a resisting foe.

Is it a good beginning to such end

To slaughter one who hath no furniture

Of self-defence, and him a countryman ?

Great Odin's hall, ye hold it for a truth,

Will open to feast those, and only those,

Who fall in combat 'neath a warrior's sword.

And would ye slay a youth who yet may live

To do great deeds to raise the name of Denmark,

And die bemoan'd of earth, and loved of Heav'n—

Loved most by him whom now ye think to serve,

Yet rob him of a worthy worshipper ?

Give me this life, brave men ! and let me boast

This happy prelude to still better things,

And by Northumbria's long-sought crown I swear,

And by my hate of English Athelstan,

That I will yield myself a sacrifice

Unto this coward mallet, should I fail

To give our Odin ten grown lives in change

For this poor child's—ten Saxons fairly slain.

Those victims, friends ! most please the god of war,

Made in the field on which he looks from high

To see the game of life play'd gallantly,

When soldiers risk the loss of what they strive

To win from others, sword defying sword,

Strength pressing strength, and man opposed to man!"

O'er Helna's face what shades of feeling swept,

As thus the young Prince spake—more bold it was

To speak such words, than front a hundred foes.

" He loves a Christian !" with a mutter'd hate

She cried, then look'd upon him steadily,

But hated less the longer that she look'd.

And as a film of ice, form'd hastily,

Melts at the upright aspect of the sun,

So softer feelings flow'd in life and warmth

Before the noble ardour of his face.

Slowly toward the stone she stept, and raised

The boy from off it, bidding him depart ;

And the stern soldiers, wisely smiling, said,

That only Anlaf, with his surplusage

Of bravery and of beauty, could have touch'd
The haughty spirit of the Prophetess.

But the young boy, before he went, fell down
At Anlaf's feet, and ask'd to be his slave ;
And ever after, follow'd him about,
To hand him aught he needed in the fight,
To furnish aught he wish'd for in repose,
With faithful watchings and obedient love.

In London sat King Athelstan, and held
Deep counsel with his Thanes, a chosen few.
Good counsellors were they, whose only thought
Was to meet force with force, and save the pride
Of England, crushing those who trod on it—
Power was the means, and the best policy
To give it vantage how to act the best.
From every part the king cull'd arms and men,
Where such fruit could be gather'd, and had sent
All studied elements of war to York,

Thinking therein in time to concentrate

The thunder ere it brake ; and he himself

Would follow last and best, and head th' assault

And to their ocean drive the sea-dogs back,

Or die a death to glorify defeat.

His calm and vigilant boldness (with the love

Of the old game of fighting) won e'en those

Who long had hated him in heart to cry

"'Tis a brave leader !   They who'd follow him

Need not to think how best they can get back.

A merit this to outvote many faults,

However loudly they cry 'down with him !'"

Then, as in thought the martial council sat

Straining for action, one gain'd access there

Who came with news, a messenger from where

Saxon and Dane in bloody grappling met,

And cried "O king !   The Danish hosts have trod

The herbage on the Humber's banks to dust ;

And as they march in countless bands, the air

Is surfeited with oaths, and vaunting cries.
One band—" and here he stopt, but Athelstan
Shouted aloud "Speak on !" and thus he spake,
" One bears a banner where is writ in red,
Revenge for Edwin, and for Æthelward !"
Then over the king's face was drawn a look
Of faintness as a veil, and on his brow
Stood out great drops, the children of distress,
And if 'twas fear that caused them ne'er before
Had fear surprised the soul of Athelstan.

And when the sun for one half-hour had left
Mid-heav'n, there came a second messenger
Who cried, " O king !   God give the victory
Unto thy troops !   But those fell wolves of war,
The Danish robbers, overweigh our men
In numbers that Death thins not.   When they fall—
For thousands fall—more seem to gain more strength.
Fired by the sight, and on with fiercer yell,
They come like wild beasts on the guarded fold,

O'erleaping every fence of opposition.

Alas! that for each Saxon flag that floats

Ten foreign banners sweep the upper air :

Our glory and its emblems lie in dust!"

In the king's face, as spake the messenger,

There was a perilous look of smother'd flame.

The broad-knit muscles of his hand swell'd up,

And the hard fingers open'd out and shut,

As they would circle something, and then tear it,

Easily, when they will'd, in fitting time.

But he spake not, and on his countenance,

The fearless Thanes look'd with a silent fear.

Hours past without another messenger.

But when the air grew melancholy grey

Beneath the fall of night, and human minds

Borrow'd the colours of the sombre sky

To tint their thoughts with, there approach'd a third

To that old Hall, whose low thick-pillar'd roof

Was lit by torch-lights that contested it
With the desponding day—slowly he trod,
Slowly, and droopingly—so look'd he, asking
By looking leave to speak. "Speak!" cried the king.
And then he spake. "All's lost! The victory
Is with the Danes and Anlaf. Constantine,
The Scottish king, has join'd the conquerors."
Up with a passionate spring King Athelstan
Rose, and he cried a low and bitter cry
As if with the mere hatred of his soul
He would destroy each Dane from English soil.
And next, more loudly. "We possess the son
Of Constantine for hostage. Bring him here!"

They found him sitting at the evening meal,
And raising up the wine—down as they spake
Dropt the loosed goblet, and the red pool spread
Like new-shed blood on the unwounded board.
And as they brought him, they enlarged upon
The news that had a bitter savour in it,

Tasting of death—but who can tell his time ?

Oft the most imminent hazard that we fly

Leaves skin and bone unscathed, while what we brave

With careless courage, sinks us to the feet

Of the one king whom not a subject loves.

But when his looks fell on the royal look,

Made e'en more terrible, as seen and hid

By light and shade alternate dappling it,

His spirit fainted.   Then spake Athelstan,

' Thy sire hath join'd the foe—that was well done—

And, better still, hath past from his sworn word ;

And best of all, poor princeling ! hath left thee

To pay the penalty of his defect !

Then hear our vengeance.   Thou art free ! Begone !

And tell him—tell his gentle Danish friends—

We rate too low the value of a life

From such a stock to be at pains to take it.

Father or son—one, millions—Pagan, Christian,

Let all come—nay by Heav'n, we'd send them men

To swell their numbers, could such things be found

For such a duty—but we'll sweep the dust
Of this invasion from our English land,
Till not the presence of one Dane or Scot
Shall with its villanous impurity
Infect the freedom of our atmosphere !
Go ! ;" and he look'd all England in himself,
And his face seem'd to cast out sparks from it,
Struck by his glorious passion.   Lowly down
All bent before him, subjected in soul
To nature's monarch, the man Athelstan.

With a great host, all those whom glory urged
Or diligence could gather, northward march'd
The patriot monarch.   Quick they were to march,
But not so quick as was their leader's wish.
Devouring the mid distance, his desire
Went forward to that final battle-field,
The bloody lists where two strong nations arm'd
From heel to crest would meet in mortal shock.
The forceful spirit of King Athelstan

Balanced the stake to be contested for,

In all its greatness—England's native life!

But ere he went, he summon'd Eadgitha,

And counsell'd safety in the distant shades

Of some poor abbey, as her purpose ran,

If safety could inhabit the same land

Where dwelt in power the sacrilegious Dane.

The mild small prettiness of Eadgitha

Was heighten'd into beauty, as she swell'd

In mien and stature, proudly answering him,

" I am the sister of King Athelstan,

King Edward was my sire, and Alfred *his!*

Here will I stay.   Here may I be of use,

For aid, for news, for death,—but not for flight!"

Out cried the king, " By Heaven such sentiments

Are worth a score of abbeys—not " and here

He spake with reverence—" not that they are not

Heav'n's houses upon earth.   God hold them safe

'Gainst the pollution of unchristian dogs!"

Northward and northward on he march'd, and then

Turning he came near Beverley,* and there

With steps slow-paced, and weariness of eye,

And with a look as if they did not think

Of many things, but thought incessantly

Of the one thing they thought of, on the road

Some pilgrims met him, self-sufficient men,

Who had no need of gold or silver store,

Or sounding names, or change of many robes,

Or trappings to adorn their sanctity.

---

* The worthy chronicler Æthelred in his " Genealogy of the Kings
of England," p. 357, informs us that when King Athelstan was on
his way to the North, he met in the province of Lindesay, a crowd
of mendicants, of whom he inquired whence they came, and was
told they had been to pay their devotions at the shrine of St. John
of Beverley. Being quite in the humour to dialogue with devotees,
he inquired whether they had ever derived any advantage from the
worship of the Saint, and was assured by one of the ragged palmers
that having been blind from his birth, he had been restored to sight
by the wonder-working power of the Beverley Bones. A second
went on to relate that he had been lame from his mother's womb,
until the visit to Beverley, when his walking powers became equal
to those of any other man. After relations so startling, the king
could do no less in his turn, than pay his devotions at the vaunted
shrine, where he left his dagger in pawn, and afterwards redeemed
it with magnificent and costly gifts to the monks, who knew how to
subsist in affluence upon the credulity and folly of their contem-
poraries.

"Whence come ye?" cried the king.   "From wor-
    shipping
St. John of Beverley," they said, "His shrine,
We know no greater."   "Want ye anything
A king can do for you?" quoth Athelstan.
"Kings can give nothing but what springs from earth,"
They answer'd, "and is earthy.   'Tis this weight
Of earth that hangs upon our limbs, and keeps
The spirit from the home which it desires.
It is earth's joys and its necessities,
Which dim and dazzle mortal eyes, and hold
Their insight from the scene of purer things;
Which taint the senses of the soul, till taste
And smell and hearing have no aptitudes
For apprehending immortality."
It was a sorrowing gaze which Athelstan
Bent on these men, whose virtue-balanced minds
Made of less weight the jewels of a crown,
Than the least leaflet of the smallest flower
That grew in Paradise.   "Ourselves will go

To Beverley," he cried ; and went.   'Twas night.

It was the hour of silence and of ease,

When to the monastery of St. John

The monarch with his intimate warriors

Repair'd for worship, and to vow a vow.

Rude swinging lamps lit hastily, just show'd

Th' imperial train, slow-pacing up the aisle,

More soldierly than royal in its pomp.

And when King Athelstan, the great, had reach'd

To the high altar, he bent down his head,

And buried it in his capacious hands.

Unto himself, and long and silently

He pray'd, and silent all the monks stood round,

And silent each mail-breasted warrior stood :

And the lamps ceased to rattle and to flare,

And the wind hush'd its low monastic voice.

But when the King unclosed his countenance,

All, seeing, wonder'd what the thoughts must be

That could so greatly vex so great a man.

So one might see, and tremble as he saw,

A cloudy mountain, alp or apennine,

Heaved by volcanic torture from its roots.

   Unclasping next the dagger from his waist

He laid it on the altar, praying out

For all to hear, " If victory leads me back

Again to tread within this home of God—

For never will I tread here else, ne'er thrust

Upon a Christian fane the spectacle

Of its successless champion—here I vow

To buy this dagger back with royal gifts

Befitting one who from his country's soil

Hath swept his country's foe, and thus becomes

Worthy to rule the people he hath freed.

Then shall the world flock hitherward to view

This temple of St. John of Beverley.

His flag shall head our armies to the war,

And will not then the Pagan Dane recoil

Before the standard for which angels fight ?

Hear us great Saint, from thy eternal house

Not made by hands, and grant what thou dost hear!

Thou didst love England, her we strive to save—

Thou hatest heathens, them we seek to crush!"

Turning, the King's sword in a salient foot

Of the high altar caught, and forward threw

His weight, half-overbalanced from its poise.

His bold attendants started at the sight

As ominous of ill, but Athelstan

Cried, "'Tis a good rebuke to us who stood

Uttering a vow which claim'd our knees to plead

Its acceptation—let us kneel to crave

Heaven's favour for a fault repaired, and hope

Grace for a vow repeated with more grace."

Then the cowl'd monks thought Athelstan was wise,

And the mail'd chiefs thought Athelstan was brave.

And all knelt down, and solemnly the King

Vow'd his first vow, and pray'd his prayer, with voice

Untrembling, as his heart was, when he struck

With his sharp sword at England's enemies.

And when he ended, some say a strange light

Shone through the nave, as if the Saint had smiled

Upon the offering ; yet 'twas possibly

The lamp-beams backward cast in glistening waves

From shaven crown, and iron-helmeted head,

As all rose up from the unmatted stone.

Then down the holy avenue they paced

Their homeward way, affronting with spurr'd heel,

And jangling arms, its solid peacefulness.

High held the Thanes their martial heads so soon

For many there to be laid low, with lips

Never again to move in pray'r to God,

Nor give their consorts a returning kiss.

BOOK VI.

THE sun was low when Anlaf and the kings

Of Cumberland and Scotland, with a cloud

Of Danes and Norsemen, and the produce bred

From his own Irish Principality,

Sat down confusedly, jealous of delay,

North of the Humber, close by Brunnaburgh.*

Flush'd, but not glutted with their past success,

* The field of Brunnaburgh is still designated by history an unknown locality, which shows how wanting in curiosity our ancient chroniclers were—for the combat fought on that obscure spot narrowly missed becoming the Assandune or Hastings of the tenth century. We cannot however avoid picturing it to ourselves as smooth and level, fitted by nature for the evolutions of great armies, and before it had been stained with gore, green as an emerald. The good old Abbot of Croyland, who admired the great men of former days, as much as he hated those of his own times— among others the dauntless Harold—is seized by an epic enthusiasm when the current of events leads him to speak of the Battle of Brunnaburgh, which has been dressed up by the imagination of our ancestors with triumphant details, and mythical incidents.

Hungry they were for victories yet unfought,

And countless as the locusts, when they clothe

With their own bodies, thicker than a fold

Of autumn nights' unseasonable snow,

From mile to mile the plains of Araby.

And within thrice the distance that a hand

Expert in handling bows from infancy

Could shoot a light-tipp'd arrow in a flight,

Was pitch'd the tent of Athelstan.   Around

Were men from Mercia and East Anglia,

West Saxons and Northumbrians, and the flow'r

Of London, fewer than the foe, but swell'd

To double numbers by the trusting hearts

They gave to their great leader's destiny.

He too had hired, by payment of good coin,

Some Vikings and their active sympathies,

Of whom were Egils, and bold Thorolf chief.

Egils was Thorolf's friend and Thorolf his—

Bound each to each by natural tastes and love

Of hearts born fearless, and hands train'd to strike.

The sun had fall'n from sight when Athelstan

Sat in his tent with disencumber'd heart ;

For he had set its place to every thing,

As much as might be in the days when art

Made not, as now, each man an atom plann'd

To swell the guided impulse of the whole.

Ev'n with a calm and stern delight he dwelt

Upon the morrow, for his mind could raise

A bulwark against danger, and then rest,

While his soul fail'd not if the bulwark fell.

Musing he sat.   It was the banquet-room.

Nail'd to the poles oil-nurtur'd lamp-pans cast

A flick'ring light upon the feasting Thanes,

But sparingly the clear-brain'd monarch ate

The viands scatter'd o'er the solid board,

Which none pass'd by as he, and sparingly

He quaff'd at times the thought-confounding bowl.

So while he mused a wand'ring minstrel came,

And sought to show his powers of touch and song.*

Young was he, tall, slight, straight and sinewy ;

With a frank look, where boldness shared the half

Of the bronzed face with prudent intellect.

Setting his small harp on the naked ground,

O'er its four strings he ran his rapid hand,

And slightly bowing to the King's consent,

Swept off at once into the tide of song.

Thor miss'd his hammer one luckless day,

   'Twas a mortal loss to him—

And Loki said it was hid away

   In the house of the giant Thrym.

And he had sworn by his own grey head,

   To keep it as safe as life,

* The adventure attributed to the Northumbrian prince is obviously an imitation of that which the chroniclers are fond of recounting of the great and heroic Alfred, the interest in whose story is positively damaged by injudicious repetition. Had the events of those times been regulated by poetical justice, this son of a patricidal father would have worsted his fratricidal rival and snatched from him the crown of England. But his night visit in disguise to the English camp could not be made to rival that of Alfred at Ethandune, and the danger in which he placed himself produced no happy fruits.

Till Thor himself to the giant's bed
    Should send his goddess wife.

Now Freyja hated the thought like Hell,
    Her husband hated it too.
And they said to Loki the Wise, " O ! tell
    The thing that is best to do."

Quoth Loki to Thor, " First lay aside
    Thy dress, and from Freyja's store
Choose out the robes that befit a bride,
    And then will I tell thee more."

The giant sat in his house at noon,
    Watching with anxious face,
For he hoped to clasp in Freyja soon
    A bride of immortal race.

And Loki, he brought her there at last—
    She was tall and huge to see—
And he cried, as the giant look'd aghast,
    " She's a noble wife for thee !"

She ate at once, like a single sop,
    A meal for a hundred men :
And seizing a wine-cask full to the top,
    To the dregs she drank it then.

The giant peep'd at his beauteous prize,
    Round her long bridal veil ;
And he started back, as from two great eyes
    Flew sparks like a fiery hail.

Cried he, " I never 'neath female brow,
    Saw eyes that had such a glow !"
Then answer'd Loki, " Thrice happy thou !
    It is that she loves thee so.

Now bring the hammer to her, great Thrym !
    Thou hast sworn it by thy might.
And with it I'll hasten back to him
    To whom it belongs by right."

The love-sick giant his hammer brought,
    And he laid it on her knee ;
Then up as quick as a flash of thought
    Sprang Thor, for the bride was he.

He grasp'd the hammer, and swung it round,
　　And he laugh'd with all his main,
Till the tall house rock'd with the awful sound,
　　And he swung it round again,

And it fell like a bolt of thunder down
　　On the giant's grisly head,
And he lay there, cleft from chin to crown.
　　'Twas a bloody marriage-bed !

Pleased with the strain, the music-loving king
Heard out the song, and then commanded more.
" Nay," cried the minstrel, but he check'd himself
In his brief utterance, veiling with a smile
A look like discontent.　Again, he sang
And pleased again, and thus the ditty ran.

Duke Hastings was a warrior bold as Normandy e'er saw,
His arguments were pointed spears, his battle-axe was
　　law,
He coursed about the ocean with a hundred ships in
　　train,
And richly plunder'd all the coasts of Africa and Spain

He came to Luna's city, raised by old Etruscan men ;

It was the feast of Christmas-tide, and all made merry
then.

But Luna was a city built with sea-walls high and
thick,

He could not enter there by force, and so the Duke
fell sick.

And after many days had past, a rumour wide was
spread,

That Hastings had grown worse and worse, and next
that he was dead.

And from the city-walls they heard, ascending to the
sky,

A hundred ships with flags depress'd, pour out a wailing cry.

Next morning unto Luna came an envoy from the fleet,

Charged strictly all its citizens with cordial words to
greet ;

And tell them that the duke had died repenting of the
past,

And with the faith which he had spurn'd on friendly
terms at last.

So to the Church of Christ he will'd to leave his wealth
    entire,

And scape, perchance, Hell's punishment, a brand from
    out the fire,

If but the Bishop would permit his corpse be brought
    on shore,

And buried in some temple there beneath its holy
    floor.

The Bishop blest God's providence, and gladly gave
    consent,

And gladly to his vessel back the Norman envoy
    went.

The next day a long funeral-train, with coffin and with
    pall,

Weeping and bosom-beating stood before the city-wall.

The gates were ope'd, and through they march'd with
    slow and solemn pace,

Each mourner in large flowing robe, and holding down
    his face ;

And Luna's citizens stood by to see the train pass on

To where the old Cathedral high in painted beauty
    shone.

Down in the middle nave they set the coffin with a
ring,
And then the pall began to move as 'twere a human
thing,
And from beneath it suddenly the stout Duke Hastings
rose,
A living warrior arm'd, and not a corpse in funeral
clothes.

His mourners all raised up their heads, and let their
robes fall down,
And stood in battle-panoply array'd from heel to crown.
The Bishop and his clergy turn'd, and fled with idle
screams,
For on the old Cathedral floor, their blood soon flow'd
in streams.

The Duke into the city then, with all his followers ran,
And quickly they with sword and axe slew every fight-
ing man.
Thus Luna, proud of old renown, was taken by a trick,
Though all its citizens were brave, and all its walls
were thick.

" 'Tis a good song," cried Athelstan, " and hath

The same plot as the first, to make of fraud

A pander unto force—yet 'twas well sung."

Then did the king bid fetch a purse of gold,

And cast it in the ballad-chanter's lap.

Can gold e'er fail to please ? but so it was ;

He handled it as though he liked it not.

Yet 'twas a handsome guerdon.   And he left

The royal presence, looking as he went,

Slowly, around ; and when he stood without,

Turning, he paused and gazed, and gazed and paused.

Ay ! 'twas a noble sight, the tent that held

In its draped folds the soldier and the king,

Whose head and hand could win a diadem,

And hold it 'gainst all comers on his brow.

Then too, to see him sit there placidly,

Him, whom the morn would light, an earthly Jove,

To hurl the bolts of battle on the foe !

So one might gaze upon a cloud wherein

The thunder sleeps in short serenity.

But off the minstrel strode with angry strides,

And, when the camp look'd buried in the dusk,

He seized the golden gift, and cast it down

Upon the vulgar earth disdainfully ;

Next, bending low, with hasty dagger scoop'd

A hole in the damp soil, and hid therein

The treasure which the world goes mad to gain.

Yet was not Heav'n so niggard of its light

But that a soldier spied the furtive deed—

One who had seen the minstrel's face of old,

Remembering what he saw.   Watching he stood.

Then turning, sought out Athelstan, and cried,

" He who did sing to thee, O King ! to whom

Thou didst give gold, and send him safe away,

Know'st thou who 'twas ?—'Twas Anlaf !"—and the king

Repeated " Anlaf !" and with sudden fit

Jerk'd out his hand, as to lay hold of him.

" How dost thou know him ? Wherefore didst thou not

Proclaim him to us ?"—and he rose in wrath.

But the man said, " I served the Danish Prince

In my vocation as a soldier once,

Not as a spy.   Him I could not betray,

And thee I've told what thou may'st profit by."

Though the king frown'd, he answer'd not ; the times

Gave sanction to rude speech, nor could he spare

One who fought well, and dared to speak the truth.

So, summoning his attendants, he bade strike

The royal tent, and pitch it further off

Some hundred paces—'twas an ominous spot

To sleep on, where his foe so late had stood,

And might breed evil dreams—this done he cast

His limbs on a hard couch, his arms at hand,

And thought of victory, smiling as he slept.

'Twas scarcely midnight when the sound of hoofs

Came clattering through the camp—but the king slept.

Next, there was noise of groaning ropes pull'd taut

By shouting men ; and pegs on whose broad heads

The heavy mallet lighted with a thud.

But 'mid the neighings, and the cries, and creaks

Of a fresh bustle, still the monarch slept.

'Twas Sherbourne's Bishop with his followers,

Who came to camp.   A sturdy militant

He was in war, yet relish'd peaceful joys.

Knowing the code of Christianity,

He hated fraud, and could distinguish well

Between the foreign wine of genuine growth,

And bastardy of home similitude.

A double-soul'd and double-handed man,

To pray or fight ; sign blessings on a head,

Or curse its wearer ere he cleft it through !

His tunicle of rich gold stuff was edged

With bells of silver ; silver bells too hung

To his long stole at either end, and these

Went tinkling, tinkling, as he swept along.

The gallant priest sought out, to pitch his tent,

A level spot, whereon was place to lodge

The multifold companions of his trip,

Heav'n's sacred things, and earthly provender ;

And found it there where Athelstan's had been.

And so 'twas pitch'd.   But not at once he sought

His wadded pallet, but first strove to lay

The thirst and hunger which the road had raised.

Then did he stretch himself in bed, and close

And ope his eyes, and sigh luxuriously,

And stretch again, as loth in sleep itself

To lose the pleasure of foretasting sleep.

Soon Nature solved the doubt, and gently wrapp'd

Her arms around him, and with motherly hand

Excluded outward objects from his sense.

Not yet the silent sky was stirr'd by light

When a sharp sound of arms brake suddenly

From near the Bishop's tent,* a mingled rush

* The eulogists of Athelstan are compelled, in describing the night before the battle, to narrate an incident which reflects but little credit on their hero's chivalry. Having been warned by the soldier who detected Anlaf through his disguise, he removed his own tent from the place of danger, but permitted the Bishop of Sherbourne, who came up late with his contingent, to occupy it without the least notice. Before morning he accordingly paid the penalty of his master's reserve.

Of cries and shuffling feet, and rapid blows.

Up at the crash of arms sprang Athelstan,

And with bare weapon seized confusedly,

Flew to the spot, to see the outermost

Of an arm'd band retreating where the night

Raised a dark wall betwixt the foe and him.

Entering the tent o'er forms of wounded men,

There lay the Bishop's body motionless

Upon his pleasant couch.   A sword-cut stretch'd

Across the jovial face (which rather show'd

Surprise than fear, so suddenly the deed

Was done, and done too well) and let the blood

Stream out of it, as red-skinn'd wine may pour

In forced libations from a jug that's crack'd.

Short time the royal warrior had to waste

Upon a corpse, but, turning off, he thank'd

For his mistake, in brief uncourteous phrase,

The ballad-monger of the eve before.

Sleep fled in terror at the sounds, to none

Returning then, to many never more.

Some to their feet sprang, rattling in the arms

In which they'd rested.   Others flew to seize

Two-handed swords, huge, sharp ; or wooden clubs,

Like hedgehogs bristling with their quills of steel ;

Or held their bucklers forward in defence,

Dreaming the foe was on them in the dark.

There was a rush of searching thro' the night,

And voices raised to answer less than ask.

And above all there thunder'd frequent cries

Of chieftains calling on their followers' names ;

Then the responsive tramp of followers.

It was a scene of terror indistinct,

Like a large picture view'd by twilight, soon

To come out boldly with the rising morn.

But then commenced, in the low eastern sky

The ever-circling war of Light with Night.

Faint, pearly beams, the arrows of the day

Shot from the far horizon, and spread round

Wider and wider, arch-wise, till at length

They conquered the whole Heav'n to their own hue.

While streaks of yellow and of crimson, flung

From the great orb beneath Earth's visible edge,

Resembled streaming blood, and flags display'd,

The fruit of battle and its instruments.*

* The defeat of Ahrimanes by Oromasdes has been synchronic
with the commencement of a thousand battles. The dawn—soft,
golden, and beautiful, which should usher in the pleasing labours of
the field, and awaken the birds to their matins—has been too often
called to witness the shedding of blood in torrents. The use of
history is to warn nations that no precautions are superfluous which
aid in keeping away enemies from their territories. England, more
than most countries, though incessantly devastated of old by invaders, has enjoyed the inestimable blessing of internal peace and
freedom from foreign encroachment. She cannot indeed boast with
Sparta of a five hundred years' exemption from the sight of an
enemy's camp-fires, but we have been so long accustomed to believe
our shores inviolable, that we may, for that very reason, omit some
time or another, to take the steps necessary for rendering them so.
I have already alluded to the facility experienced by all kinds of
buccaneers in making good a landing in England, where there existed
few fortresses or strong castles to check the advance or harass the
rear of an enemy. The Romans, those great masters of fortifica-
tion, rendered so strong the cities they left behind them in Britain,
that after the Teutonic barbarians had for ages possessed themselves
of the open country, their undisciplined hordes found themselves
totally unable to reduce the cities and larger towns. When at
length, however, they succeeded, down went the fortifications
through utter neglect of keeping them in repair, so that on the
arrival of the Danes, there existed very little in the whole land to
arrest their progress. This, in a great measure explains the difficulties of Alfred, and the earnest policy of his son Edward to stud the

But not an eye 'mid all had time to greet

The glorious birth of dawn, which only rose

To light the path of slaughter.   'Twas the hour

When buds the harvest of the blue-vein'd steel,

Where Fate and Death are reapers.   On they came,

The Danish troops, voracious to indulge

The cruel greed of war.   In mighty mass

Their centre moved, triangularly set

Upon the field, a pyramid of men.

The English monarch ranged his scantier force

To make one soldier do the work of two

By vantage of position : on the right

Thorolf, the friendly Viking, led the fight,

To whom a Saxon body join'd its strength.

kingdom with castles, which Athelstan, however, as we have already seen, was far from imitating. By degrees the Northumbrians shut themselves up in walled towns, and at intervals erected forts and castles along the coast, but never in sufficient numbers or strength to oppose any effectual impediment to an invader.   Hence the perpetual influx of those vast armaments from the Northern ocean, which, penetrating southward, subdued Mercia, East Anglia, and ultimately Wessex itself, and had the battle of Brunnaburgh taken a different turn, would have rolled across the Humber, and placed Anlaf, in diademmed state, within the ancient palace of Winchester.

The men of London, and the Mercians
Form'd firmly on the left wing ; at their head
March'd the good Chancellor, gallant Turketyl.
The van was trusted to bold Thorolf's friend
The Viking Egils ; fronting Anlaf stood
In the mid army, like a core of strength,
The soldier's confidence, King Athelstan,
Back'd deeply by the Saxons of the West.

Behind the Danish right there stretch'd a wood
Of thick extent, whose ancient trees had oft
Had their own battles with the thunder-cloud ;
But bare and level was the plain in front.
Then burst the conflict into horrid life,
And spread like a devouring flame, which strikes
With its red flaky javelins, the dry wood
Of summer boughs unvisited by rain.
So onward in impetuous multitudes
Came Dane on Dane, like wolf impelling wolf.
The beasts of earth, and elements of Heav'n

Join'd in the contest.   Breast-plated in steel
Horse rush'd on horse, with all the hate of man,
Fighting with teeth and fore-arm.   Then the South
Leagued with the East, sent forth a clamorous wind
That bent the tree-heads down, and whirl'd the dust
From myriad treaders, like a flinty mist.
While overhead the cloudy potentates
That wrapt the tempest in their vapory folds,
Met in mid Heaven, and bellow'd as they clash'd.

But equal rose the soul of Athelstan
To the high call made on it—mid the shock,
Of personal conflict, or quick transference
Of thought to action—to direct a mass
Of thousands in aggression or retreat ;
To succour yielding friends, or dash a blow
At foes too prominent ; nor hand nor head
Were wanting to the king ; and head and hand
Did their vocation calmly.   As might one,
A master in his peaceful art, direct

Some modern students of Terpsichore,

So ruled the king that bloody dance of death.

Bold Thorolf plunged into the central fight,

Shouting a cry of joy (so shouts a youth

Immersed in his best pastime) and the waves

Of battle closed around him ; still arose

His war-cry, heard by all, as men have heard

From a ship hidden in th' Atlantic trough

Her captain's voice above the watery din ;

But then it ceased, as stops the sailor's cry

When down his throat the sea-rush stifles it.

His comrade Egils mark'd him where he pierced

Into the crowd, and watch'd for his return,

And waited, but he came not, and again

He watch'd, and waited, but he did not come.

Then suddenly he saw his standard, known

By the blue eagle with out-spreading wings,

Pass flutteringly by in full retreat.

By this he felt that Death had paralysed

The arm of Thorolf, and he threw himself

With his whole force of followers on the foe.

Thus when a mass of snow immense breaks down

From side of sloping Alp, where'er it falls

It fills all space, and leaves no life beneath.

So Egils crush'd the foe—and when he found

Bold Thorolf slain, and Adils standing near,

Flouting the corpse of his dishonour'd friend,

He sprang upon him, casting down his sword,

As if a short death were too pitiful,

And grasp'd him round the neck, and prest the links

Of his strong iron shirt into his throat,

Holding him thus, until the life-pulse stopt,

Then cast the body from him with a curse.

Next Turketyl,* the gallant Chancellor,

* The chronicler of England dwells with peculiar pleasure on the achievements of chancellor Turketyl, who, exchanging the battle-axe for the rood, closed his eyes in the sanctuary of the Fens, as an abbot, almost as a saint. His life, for the details of which the reader must be referred to the history of the times, strikingly illustrates the social condition of England. He was of royal blood, and by the exertion of a skilful policy, might perhaps have had a fair

His lofty stature wrapt in battle-net,

And brandishing an ashen javelin,

Made head against the troops which Constantine

Led on in person, aided by his son.

The son and father join'd their strength as join'd

They were by blood, and co-directed aims,

And natural love, and struck at Turketyl,

Bearing him backward.   Then in timely help

Singin advanced with whirling battle-axe,

And swung it down on the young Prince's head,

Making through helm and brain a wedge-shaped gap

From which a bloody fountain spurted up:

"Now thanks to Athelstan the king," he cried,

"Who spared thee for my blade—great comfort this

If thou could'st feel it!"   But the youth fell back

Into his father's arms; his gory head

Hung sideways on the breast of Constantine,

chance of ascending the throne; but he preferred the quiet of the
cloister, where he enjoyed the conversation of literary men, who
could perhaps regale his fancy with legends of the far East, or those
incidents in the "tale of Troy divine" of which our ancestors were
peculiarly enamoured.

Who with a wond'ring horror look'd at it,

As if complaining that e'en riskful war

Had such a fate in store for him as this—

Then rais'd he up his dead child, him who was,

Alas ! who was, how short a time ago,

The purest joy his shrewd heart knew—but now !—

Away ! weep afterwards, old man ! so he

Tenderly raised him, propp'd by faithful friends,

And, sick in spirit, fled the hateful field.

Anlaf search'd every crowd for Athelstan ;

The broad orb of the Prince's shield was mark'd

By some few dents, but harmless ; convex-shaped,

And iron-beaten, on it cones of gold

Were studded, ranged in intercrossing curves ;

His helmet shone uncloven to the sun,

Its gilded dome unbreach'd by axe or sword,

And with its insolent crest, that seem'd to cry,

" Who dares touch me, must dare the consequence !"

And gladly Athelstan had found the Dane

But would not seek him; for the leader's soul

Was forced to sweep the round of circumstance,

And centralise all points to one design.

But they met once; then Anlaf seeing him

Shriek'd out, " Now ghosts of Æthelward and Edwin.

Look on !"   A fiery hatred seem'd to burn

The very visage of king Athelstan—

" Ha ! by St. John of Beverley !" he cried,

And with a bound of strength unnatural leapt

Upon the Danish Prince, following whose steps

Was the young boy whom he had saved from death,

A sacrifice to Odin—back he fled,

Scared by the flashing of the Saxon blade.

But Helna, who was near (for through the fight

With voice and gesture prominent she moved,

And quicken'd action with prophetic cries),

Saw the descending death, and thrust herself

Before the sword-blow—gash'd in neck and breast

Down dropt she.   Well it was for life that thus

The full swing of that dreadful sword was check'd

By the small interval at which she stood
Betwixt the King and the young Prince : again
Down fell that murderous blade, and cleft the shield
Of Anlaf, gold and iron both, and pierced
Half through his helmet, forcing him recoil
Ten paces backward, the fierce Saxon king
Exclaiming as he struck, " Not yet enough
I've paid thee for thy songs."   But round them closed
The stormy crowd of foes and followers.

    No longer then with quiet fearlessness
Moved Athelstan from point to point, but raged
Lion-like, when the animal majesty
Is bearded ; so he desperately ran
At every show of hostile armoury,
Whether it cased a hundred men or one—
And at his side his brother Edmund strove,
Young in war's honours, to keep pace with him.
Thus a cub-tiger, when its royal sire
Chases for food the swift-heel'd antelope,

Hangs on his flying stride with emulous strides.

Missing their leader's clue, the men he led

Grew wild at first, then waver'd, and some turn'd

Ready to fly; and England seem'd to lose

The heart oracular of victory;

While the fierce Dane, and his commingled mass

Of peoples, came tumultuously on,

Furious at the long stop which time had set

To their advance, but which at last appear'd

To leave clear pathway to the deluging stream.

Yet flow'd it not uncheck'd, for even they

Less bold by nature, from close neighbourhood

With fighters caught the rage of fight, and propp'd

The greater combatants who sullenly

Refused defeat.   But Anlaf burnt to do

Some deed befitting one now half a king;

And leagued with Constantine (who once again

Had join'd the battle), thrust so heavily

Upon the English centre, that it bent

And crumbled, as a wall might, vex'd beneath

The swingings of the brazen catapult.

This saw the gallant Chancellor Turketyl,

And gathering up his force, he call'd in aid

The Viking Egils with his glorious band,

And a stout monk of Croyland (Athelstan

To Croyland's monastery of his grace

Had given the first-made set of English bells).

Then swept they round by a long sinuous path

Behind the swell of an uneven ground

Which, rough with ragged stones and dusty shrubs,

Rose desolate and morose. With tread unheard

Save by themselves, they gain'd the furthest flank

Of the deep wood, and through its shelter wound

Their rapid way. The autumn sun ahead,

Climbing the sloping plain of peaceful Heav'n,

Shone on their backs emerging from the trees,

Like a broad torrent broken up by rocks.

Forming, they gain'd the rear of the mix'd bands

Of Constantine and Anlaf, loosely spread

Like men disorder'd by their happiness.

On these in one dense wedge, and with one soul,

The troops of Turketyl and Egils fell,

With the stout monk of Croyland well in front,

And drove themselves from back to front right through

The hostile crowd, leaving a path behind

Broad, clean, save where 'twas cumber'd by dead men.

Thus through an Indian field, the beating hail

Forces a road-way wide of level grain,

Whose sides are bounded by the standing corn.

Then turning round, they, with their force and hate

Sharpen'd by triumph, swept a second lane

Through the bewilder'd foe, and as they paused,

Concentrating their fearful elements

For the third onfall, royal Athelstan,

Catching the vantage, hurriedly closed up

With the West Saxons and the Londoners ;

And, like a waterfall in sheer descent

Of half a thousand feet, precipitously

Dash'd on the Danish front.   The foe, hard held

As in the iron jawbones of a vice,

Were bloodily crush'd ; but few found room to fly ;

And these did worse than if they there had left

Their life and limbs, for to their farthest friends

They spread contagion both of fright and flight.

Success itself, the Dane's late gain, became

His means of loss ; for fear, which jumps at ends

O'er logical interval, suggested plots,

And feign'd defeats, which bend more easily

To rise victorious : this timidity,

Enlarged to panic, took the general heart,

As great and fierce as was its vaunting trust.

Prince Anlaf for a while stood haughtily

Awaiting death, as willing on that spot

To lay himself and his imperial hopes,

When raising upward his blood-blinded eyes

He saw a vision, or he seem'd to see—

'Twas Bertha.   Pedestall'd on air, she held

A cross in her left hand, and with the right,

Beckon'd him to her.   With fresh-blooded hope,

Up like a wild beast from the hunter's toils

He bounded from the earth, and bursting through

The growing wall of foes, built up in steel,

He found himself, scarce knowing how, without,

Borne onward in the stream of fugitives

That swell'd, and roar'd, and deepen'd as it flow'd :

For a great terror, palsying reason, seized

On the whole hostile 'multitude.   At last

The Raven standard sullenly gave way,

As unaccustom'd to that shame of war ;

(The Raven,* woven by the sisters three

Of the fierce Ragnor Ladbrok, king of ships,

---

* Speaking of a battle which took place in Alfred's time, Asser
says, "There they gained a very large booty, and among others the
standard called 'Raven,' for they say that the three sisters of
Hingwar and Hubba, daughters of Lodobrock, wove that flag and
got it ready in one day. They say, moreover, that in every battle,
wherever that flag went before them, if they were to gain the
victory, a live crow would appear flying on the middle of the flag ;
but if they were doomed to be defeated it would hang down motionless, and this was often proved to be so."—"*Life of Alfred*," p. 62 ;
vide also "*The Four Conquests of England*," i. 346.

Grandsire of Sihtric of Northumbria ;)
And Wessex' golden dragon o'er the field
Pursued the ominous bird that oft had stretch'd
Mid northern mists its desolating wings
In flight for England, and with ravaging beak
Swept down the pleasant valley of the Trent,
Or startled Sherwood forest with its cry.
Then Scotch and Kymri, Danes and Irish—all
Who had sail'd up the Humber, or had crost
The frontier line of Scotland, rioting
In conquest not yet gain'd—strew'd the long road
With many fashions of one common death.

The taste of slaughter fed the wish to slay :
So, Saxon soldiers cursed the lack of time,
Which, while they struck all laggards in the flight,
Let 'scape the foremost. Horsemen, worn with work,
In iron clothing, and in number few,
Strain'd their tired steeds to head the fugitives,
And whom they headed, none moved limb again.

Chiefly King Athelstan the Conqueror,

Son of the son of Alfred great and wise,

Hunted the foe who had pursued of old

His grandsire through the bogs of Somerset.

Like a fierce angel, terrible he rode,

With more than mortal warrant to avenge

The outrage upon England's majesty.

The Dane was scared to see his form, not great

By gift of nature, take a giant's size,

Swollen by indwelling of demoniac power;

While flying backs were shot through by his eyes,

Whence issued rays, like javelins of fire,

Giving his sword an enforced idleness.

But thundering on the way he there espied

The boy whom Anlaf saved, low lying, stain'd

By dirt and blood, with half-shut eye that shunn'd

The sight of his own wounds, and hands too weak

To ask the pity which his look implored.

The hot king stopp'd in mid career, and raised

The youth up in his arms, and in the charge

Of an old follower placed him—then, away,
Away again upon his ride of death.

With axe and sword, and every instrument
Pointed, or edged, or wing'd, the best to give
Life the worst chance of 'scaping savagely
The victors chased the savage foe, till night
Confounded objects in its merciful shades ;
And Athelstan and England slept secure.

As Anlaf on his faithful war-horse spurn'd
The road in quick retreat, from out a hut,
Thatch'd sparely with broad-breasted water-flags,
And mud-wall'd, rush'd a countryman, who spake
Some rapid words ; then Anlaf followed him.
Within the cheerless dwelling, bleeding yet,
But coarsely bandaged, lay the prophetess,
Young Helna, floor and rushes for her bed.
Her pallid beauty turn'd to red at sight
Of the young Prince, and that fierce look which still

Lorded her countenance, ev'n in this hour

Of humbled place and state, and desperate pain,

Retreated, yielding to a soften'd shame.

" I would not speak what now I speak," she cried,

" With life before me—I have seen thee once—

Once more ! 'Tis more—but go ! nay, thank me not

For my small aid.   I had no pow'r to choose.

A greater despot than my own wild heart

Master'd my acts.   Thou lov'st a Christian—go.

I cannot wish thee ill—I cannot wish

Ill befall her who will become thy joy."

Here the proud lip grew tremulous ; a tear

Crept down the cheek, which feeling ne'er before

Had moisten'd with such dew.   "No !" Anlaf said.

" I go not hence till, Helna, thou art safe.

Desert the life that bled for mine !   Such act

Would shame a Saxon soldier.   Fly with me !

Gladly my horse will bear her who braved death

To guard his master."   Answering not, and sighing,

She shook her head.   Just then a rush of sounds

Came faintly from the distance.   Helna heard,

And with an effort raised her slender form,

Exclaiming, " 'Tis the Saxon in pursuit !

Soon will the furious Athelstan be here.

Great as thou art, thou can'st not face a fiend.

Away then for thy life—for Bertha's life !

Thou wilt not stir ?   I tell thee,"—and her gaze

Shone with the dying spark of prophecy,

" I tell thee—and, this finish'd, never more

Shall I predict or good or evil—Anlaf !

Fate destines thee for empire yet, my Prince,

Northumbria waits her sovereign lord in thee.

The Gods have will'd it—why defy the Gods ?

Thy life is due to glory, love, and hate ;

Think of thyself, of Bertha, Athelstan !

Fly—let me feel ! O, let me feel at last

My love has not been useless !"   Anlaf stood

As might a victim at a sacrifice

He fears, but would not shun, then calmly said,

" Never ! I will not leave thee, while yet life

Is in thee to be guarded !"   But the sounds

Confused of hasty feet and shouts came near

And nearer, louder still, as might a storm

Advance upon some gallant ship that lies

Unmoving in the hollow windless wave,

And there, foreseeing its dark enemy,

Waits silent for the blow it cannot ward.

Then rose up Helna from her rushy bed

And crying, " Not while I live wilt thou fly ?

There—wait no longer !" and with rapid hand

She tore the wrappings from her poor maim'd limbs,

And sinking backward, such a well of blood

Gush'd from them as to wash out life at once.

Her eye, made fast on Anlaf, still retain'd

A gleam of fondness, slowly dying there

To twilight, till the gaze, tho' changing not

Its first direction, look'd a dull gem, fix'd

In a spoilt setting, cold and meaningless.

BOOK VII.

If like a huge and slowly-moving wheel

Time turns events, and bids them mount again

To their first point, this doth it do alone

For the large life of nations.   Unto man

It brings no more the blessings which he clasp'd

In the ascendant.   When they sink they die.

And so it drops the curtain on the stage

Where Youth, Strength, Hope were actors—thus it blights

The bloom of hearts as well as looks, and works

The death of feeling and the loss of love.

Movement, and work, and daylight—these are things

That make the life of thousands.   Evening falls

Too often on the men that use the world

Like a sad prophet of the coming night

When none may work ; and what that night may

          bring—

The rest of peace, or never-quiet pain—

Depends on the day's labour.   Conscience starts

At the mind's picture of the past, its scenes

Of chequer'd light, and its dark terrible shade.

And so the man of action sighs for light

And for more action, casting backward looks

On battles and on sieges, councils, plots,

And all the wheels and hum, and flash and warmth

Of moving being ; the hot blood of youth,

The well-strung muscles, and the sweatful noon ;

Then turns reluctant to the sinking sun.

   Near Abingdon, and where the wanton Ock

Is married to the Isis, Athelstan

Had built a palace on an isle, whose sides,

Though neither high nor broad, had power to fret

And to divide the down-flow of the Thames.*

Here would he sit at times, and reckon up

The glories of his country—for he knew

The hand that raised her—crying to his heart,

" Is not this England, I have made so great

And gallant for my use ?" and so it was ;

And thus to think was greatness in itself—

But the thought was not follow'd by a smile.

The conqueror was conquer'd—so it seem'd—

By uncommunicated cares. The man,

The mighty man whose front was to the fight

* Two regal delinquents, Offa and Athelstan, haunted by remorse, sought a remission of mental suffering on a holme in the Thames near Abingdon, where the great monastery founded in the reign of Ina and enriched by a long succession of kings, frowned like a vast fortress over the river and the surrounding country. Among the chronicles which have been recently disinterred and rendered accessible to historians in good fair type, that of Abingdon is one of the most interesting and valuable, tracing the fortunes of the abbey from the reign of the sanguinary Briton, Cadwalla, to that of the still more sanguinary Norman, who quenched at Hastings the early flame of English liberty. The description of such spots supplies in history a pleasant contrast with ferocious deeds of arms, and achievements in the innermost deadly breach.

In every battle, would, without a blush,
Have borne the shame of flying from himself.

Then was the council set at Abingdon,
And matters of grave import fixed their mark
Upon the looks of men who ponder'd them—
Old men and staid, whose thoughts were character'd
By the rough shrewdness, the near-sighted wit
Of a half-civilised experience.
There Eadwulf rose, a hybrid of the times
When labour of all sorts was not, as now,
Shared and sub-shared by many hands and hearts
For better doing—one-third soldier he,
And one-third priest, and one-third anything—
Rising he let his tongue run flatteringly
Upon the war successes of the king,
And counsell'd him on England's present pow'r
To raise the edifice of pow'r to come.
Then the rest said that thus the thing should be,
And that the king could do what should be done.

Further he spake of Charles the Simple slain

By the assassin's dagger at Peyronne ;

That Louis d' Outre-mer was now in England

And that his claim to fill the throne of France

Might—tho' the Carlovingian was a thing

Treacherous and false, and doubtful in its sex—

Be made a step-stone for a surer man

To set his foot on ; let the king say how.

Next Alain Barbe-tourte, savage as the beasts

Whose skin he wore, and with coarse-knotted mind

Kin to the club with which he roam'd the woods,

Might be compell'd to lend a helping hand

To win the fair domains of Burgundy.

And the rest cried that thus the thing should be,

And that the king could do what should be done.

Then spake the king in words that from his mouth

Came easily, as birds from an op'd cage,

" 'Tis not alone by armèd force of hands

That a whole country can be brought to yield

A wholesome and a pleased obedience.

The feelings of the ruled, save those alone

Who do rebel against all virtuous law,

When with the ruler's acts in unison

Give to dominion its enduring grip ;

And these can seldom be call'd forth by him

Whose seat of power lies in a foreign land

Of varied climates and strange habitudes.

But when two nations whom broad seas divide,

Or rocky range of nature-planted bar,

Are bound in ties of unforced amity,

Each unto each imparts the greatest good,

By barter'd blessings and rebound of thought.

This widens out the custom-narrow'd mind

Made capable of a larger charity ;

Thus nature's local blessings are spread out

Over a broader interchanging space,

And sever'd men are link'd unto their kind

By reciprocity of benefit.

Here I announce an instant embassy

From Hugh Le Grand.* He asks us for a wife;

And should I lend my father's child to share

The weight of his ancestral dignities,

England may bless the day that gives its king

A brother, clear of head and clean of hand."

He ceased, and each one, spite of impotence

Of mind and knowledge to embrace in whole

The royal matter, cried the king was right,

For each one thought him wiser than the rest.

Yet when he stopp'd the course of words that flow'd—

Though freighted heavily with sense, and clear,—

From out a mind that seem'd preoccupied

With other thinkings, back in his high chair

He sank with a sore spirit-thwarted look,

Like one who hungers for some dainty food,

---

* Several chroniclers, among whom William of Malmesbury deserves to be particularly noticed, have left us a description of the presents made by Hugh to Athelstan for his sister. One of these, an alabaster vase, evidently of Hellenic workmanship, is celebrated for its rare beauty. "It was," says Malmesbury, "so exquisitely chased that the corn-fields really seemed to wave, the vines to bud, figures of men actually to move; and so clear and polished that it reflected the features like a mirror."—Book ii., Ch. 6.

When o'er his soul a sudden sickness comes,
And his taste shudders at the natural joy.

And after days, by honor'd deputy
Came Hugh le Grand, the Duke of France, and brought
Rich presents with him—he himself a man
Of well-ascended years, tho' not yet reach'd
Life's summit, with a look that, calmly keen,
Seem'd to detect the future ; such a man
As in the tempting present fruit could see
The germ of evil, and forbear to pluck.
So, Hugh le Grand, of all his pleasant gifts
Sent some before, and wisely came himself
The centre of his bounty.   First appear'd
Rich robes of silk, and golden drinking-cups,
And silver-beaten things to minister
To luxury, or necessities of food.
Rare stones and perfumes with their separate gifts
Bribing the sight and smell for preference ;
And steeds that trod the ground as in disdain

To be led forth in such a peaceful show

When they had borne a warrior to the field.

Then came an ancient vase, scoop'd wond'rously

From a vast onyx, where the graver's hand

Had with a life-touch reproduced the life

Of harvest, and the merry-minded days

That illustrate the gathering of the grape.

And next rode Hugh, in delegated state,

Erect and bland.—And lest these worldly gifts

Had not enough of show and price to please,

There came such holy relics in his train

As might on the receiver's mind impress

And leave a sense of solemn thankfulness

Consistent with the boon's blest quality.

A flag of St. Mauritius led the van ;

Then on a silver tray borne delicately

A finger of that wonder-working man

St. Dionysius, excellently fresh.

Some of the nails that on the bloody cross

Had riven the limbs of Christ, claim'd reverence,

And found it from the gazers as they past.

And then a part of that strange crown—not such

As earthly monarchs wear—which tightly drew

Around the forehead of divinity

Its interlacing and assaulting thorns.

Next, in the rear, the sword of Constantine

Closed up the good procession, flaming bare,

Borne by a holy priest, as if to guard

Such heavenly treasures from the hands of earth.

It could not be but that king Athelstan

Was pleased with gifts, some fitted for the times,

And others always fit for all mankind ;

But when he saw the cruel crown of Christ,

A ruddy trembling overcame his face,

And he cried out with groans wrung audibly

To others, though himself seem'd not to hear,

Else had he check'd them, " This the diadem !

This for the end of a laborious life,—

The life of one who sold himself to death

To buy the freedom of his brotherhood ! "

But by an effort, he the royalty

Gain'd o'er himself again, and on the gifts

He look'd, and on the envoy's countenance,

And featured saw therein the elements

Of his own further rise,—and his heart rose ;

The world grew larger to him and he seem'd

To have himself a greater share in it.

So Hugh le Grand fared pleasantly, and got

Elhilda for a wife. And Abingdon

Rejoiced within its wide monastic mounds,

For from those costly gifts King Athelstan

Added yet more unto the stores that made

That house a name for wealth. And England joy'd,

And open'd all her eyes and ears to catch

The ceremonial show, and festal games

Of the great marriage, and each throat was stretch'd,

When duly mollified by wine, to praise

The royal pair who gave excuse for drink.

Excuse there wanted not for shows of skill

And feats of strength ; for tumblers twirl'd their limbs

To such contortions, that if born with them

They would have cursed the fate that made them so,

And spent their substance in appliances

To give them some humanity of form.

Men danced, and women danced, and it were doubt

If feet or throats went fastest—flinging heels

And shouting voices were the signs of joy,

And help'd each other to defy fatigue.

Drink provoked dance, and dance incited drink.

The slingers next contended for the prize.

A large fat hen was leg-tied on a post,

And he who at a hundred paces off

Knock'd the scared creature from its eminence

Would win it for his skill.   And many a stone

Dented the post, and shook the wood beneath

The hen's unwilling roost, before it fell.

At last a young man came whose scanty garb

Display'd the limbs in fatless muscle clothed,

By work, spare diet, and much open air.

Behind the bound he stood ; his right hand grasp'd

The thongs of leather, at whose lower ends

Reposed the stone within its hollow bed,

Made wider and shaped oval.   With one glance

He took the measure of the interval,

Then threw his left foot forward, whirling round

The sling at the same instant overhead.

Loosing one thong, the liberated stone

Whizz'd to the mark, and cut the slender cord

That bound the fowl ; down to the ground it fell.

A slinger caught it as it strove to fly,

And held it up, and swore it was not hit

From its perch fairly.   "Hold it !" cried the youth

"There, as thou hast it now, and if I fail

At the first throw to knock it from thy hand,

Keep it thyself, and have a second one

Which I will give thee, friend !"   Compell'd by shame

And by the jeering crowd, the man held high

The hapless fowl at arms' length from his head,

Standing with face averted.   Whistling flew
The fatal stone, and crash'd upon his hand.
Shrieking he dropt the prize, and running up
The young man pouch'd it 'mid applauding shouts.

   Next came the games of spears and javelins, cast
To cover furthest distance, or to hit
The mark—a quintain ; 'twas a wooden head,
And called "The Dane" to pleasure Athelstan.

   The course for racing stretch'd on either hand,
Rail'd in with stakes, and a grown swine the prize.
Among the runners one there was, more fleet
Than others, but with less sustaining strength.
Two brothers, well-condition'd, join'd their wits
To overreach him.   First one shot away
At his top speed to lure the swift man on
And force him to lose breath, the other waiting
With power held back to overtake and win.
But, near the goal, and when the man behind

Had closed upon his panting enemy,

The foremost brother slipt, and o'er his back

The second tumbled like a waterfall

Shooting a rock.   They, laugh'd at, in the dust,

With bloody faces sprawl'd discomfited,

And the swift runner, breathless, touch'd the goal.

Amid the many wrestlers, prominent

Was a huge Thane, the terror of the war,

Who did not think it soil'd his dignity

To try a fall with men of meaner sort.

But fall he got not, for he foil'd with ease

And with sore thumps each bold antagonist.

The last to try his fortune was the youth

Who won the prize at slings, but won not here.

The smiling giant seized him in his arms,

As might a mother dart upon her child,

And drag him from a crowd of combatants

In infant warfare ; so he carried him,

Making a show of struggling feet and hands,

To where majestic stood the well-year'd ram,

The prize of wrestling.   Gently by its side

He laid him down and cried, " Here, take the prize !

Thou hast deserved it !"   Blushing rose the youth

And bowing much, while scream'd the multitude

With joy, well primed to scream at anything.

For a short space none seem'd more sensitive

To pleasure than the king—why should the lord

Of happy men be sad ?   So, 'mid the rest

He stood up like a ruling mind embodied

Most suitably to sight, tho' somewhat worn

The frame-work seem'd ; and he unbent his state,

And spake as if mere speaking were a joy,

But look'd, unspeakingly, the first of men.

Next in the strength and spirit of his soul

He thought to try his hand, oft tried and well,

At the old games of skill and hardihood.

He seized an iron disk, and whirling it

Over his shoulder with accustom'd art,

Hurl'd the vast weight at the last limit, thinking
To overpass the bound, not used to fail.
With labour'd course the metal mass flew, falling
Short of the mark.   In body still he stood,
But o'er his face, too quick to be conceal'd,
There past the twitchings of convulsive thought,
A sad alloy of bitterness and fear ;
And men said, 'twas a grievous thing for one
To fail in aught who ne'er had fail'd before.

Then knew the king—'twas a hard thing to know ;
A lesson he had shrunk from—that his strength
Had been invaded much by penance, more
By the sharp scourge of an uneasy mind.
And when alone (too often thus alone
He was when solitude was sadness, yet
He was drawn on by an invisible force
To seek the pain he could not bear when found),
Then as it were in vision he look'd down
A long fair vista, overarch'd with green

And gay with flowers, and bright with flaring lamps,

And noisy with the shouts that hail success,

But, at the end, a small low spot of earth,

Unlit, unsounding, and unvisited,

Fit to dig holes in, and to cast in them

Dead peasants, or the carcass of a king.

A fever'd body may be soothed by art,

But what medicament can cool the mind

That blows its own consuming fire within ?

Sagacious, active, beautiful, and brave,

Against invisible darts in vain he raised

The shield of his defensive excellence ;

And every cast he made for happiness

Fell each time short and shorter of the mark.

The very greatness that he sought and gain'd,

The very good he strove to do, and did,

Were turn'd to instruments for his distress.

And a voice daily seem'd to cry at him,

"Thou art a king !   Be thankful.   Thou hast pieced

The fragments of the people into one ;

Hast caused the name of England sound abroad

With sharper ring of fame, for love or fear ;

Hast laid thy hand on princes, and hast set them

On thrones, and made thy sisters royal twice,

First in themselves, and in their husbands next.

Be happy !" and he thought, as if he gave

An answer to himself, " All this is true :

This have I done, and such I am.   The weak

Envy my lot, and the strong flatter me."

But the thought was not follow'd by a smile.

E'en gentle night deluded him with dreams

Of peaceful calm, on which his conscience lay

As on a pillow resting—then he woke

Unto the hard and real, and clamorous day.

And once he stood in thought before Heaven's walls,

Low walls of spiral fire, that seem'd to live,

And when one sought to overlook their fence,

Darted fierce flames at the intruder's face.

A gateway, but no gate, led inwardly;

And in the gap a vast bright angel stood,

Spreading his wings, shields of white adamant,

Before the entrance.   In his hand he grasp'd

A pair of scales, whose huge circumference

Held, on the one side, ponderous golden weights,

And at the other end whoever sought

To enter there might cast his claims, in view

Of bearing down the scale, and winning Heav'n.

And the king thought he had beside him bags

Of gold, and heaps of rare and precious things,

And title-deeds to wide-extended lands,

Which he had shower'd in splendid charity.

These in the scale-pan he cast eagerly,

But the remorseless balance rigid stood

High up, and bow'd not from its first estate.

Next, there was heard a din of voices, mix'd

Of prayers and blessings, offerings from the lips

Of many slaves whom Athelstan had freed.

Their breathings gather'd on the topmost scale,

Like a thick cloud—with tremulous motion down

Slightly it sank, and creak'd the balance-arm,

Prompt to descend ; but hover'd there awhile

As if uncertain, and then rising up

Stood still and pitiless, to be moved no more.

Then woke King Athelstan.   'Twas but a dream.

Why think upon a dream ? and yet he thought.

And his thoughts wasted him, and dried his strength

As the sun dries the body of a pool ;

While on his countenance an anxious look

Fought for possession with the pride that shrank

From being thought to fear for anything.

At open lattice did he sit one night.

The sun had sunk, array'd in angry red,

Mid strong environment of colour'd clouds ;

One only in the opposite heav'ns appear'd

Of a funereal black, and from its top,

As from a grave, the crescent moon emerged.

The stars were set as everlasting gems

In the deep sky and clear, clear save where patch'd
At spacious intervals by thunder-clouds,
In each of which, at times, the lightning flash'd,
Making them shine like festal palaces.
And every now and then from out their folds
Large drops of rain, the tears of evening, fell.
'Twas a strange scene, and to the king's mind seem'd
Indicative of pow'r, pow'r strong in peace,
Dwelling magnificent in quietude.
" How lives the lightning there ! " cried Athelstan,
" Doing no harm, and yet how beautiful !
And earth's success—is that but reach'd through sin ?
It must invade for conquest ; make defence
Before offence is offer'd ; sow ill seed
To gather good ; and when the crop is reap'd
It comes embitter'd by the toil and strain
Of many dark unconscientious days.
So, Pow'r and Pleasure !—let the two be pair'd,
And if they do not quarrel in their life,
One end awaits them.   Who would set a crown

Upon the bone-brow of a royal corpse?

Ay, Pow'r and happiness—all-judging God!

Why did'st thou give me the vain mind that strives

To climb these faithless heights? Praised, follow'd,
     fear'd;

But loved—how often? That were happiness!

Alas! for me, that never on my brow

Hath woman laid her sorrow-soothing palm:

Alas! for me, that never to my soul

Another gentler soul hath bound itself:

Alas! for me, a solitary star

Amid a blazing sky, whose lesser lights

Call *it* more great, but deem themselves more blest.

Power!—mockery! Hard it is to learn so late

How small is greatness unenlarged by love.

Love might—soft, wise, potential love—have saved me

From doing what I've done—what I *have* done.

What comes?" Here growing faint he call'd for help,

And lay down trembling like a child that's sick.

There did he rest awhile in sombre thought.

When, stronger grown, and lifting up his eyes,

He saw at the far room's extremity

A light most soft, but full.   'Twas not the day,

For that was in repose.   'Twas not the lamps,

For it had more of substance, and spread out

Advancing somewhat.   Gazing steadily

He saw it settle into human shape,

A silv'ry film through which the walls behind

Were visible ; and slowly, certainly,

A face smiled from it—that of Eadgitha.

It could not be, for a whole year had past

Since she had died in hopeful sanctity.

Yet there she stood !—the same, but not the same,

Like a coarse picture which an angel's hand,

Dipping its pencil in the hues of Heav'n,

Had painted o'er afresh.   He heard no voice,

Saw not a motion of her fairy lips,

Yet did it seem as if upon his brain

There were words written which his eye could read :

"All sins, tho' scarlet, may be wash'd as white
As snow-flakes in the air, but not by him
Who does the evil." Then the face died out
To the last smiling ; and the human shape
Took other shape, most like a fiery cross,
Which grew so bright he could not look on it ;
And when the eyes which he had closed perforce
Again were open'd, he saw nothing there
But earthly lamp-light flickering in the wind
And playing with the pillars and the walls.

Then strove the king, by change of place, to fly
The presence of inquisitorial care,
Which pull'd on one idea, and stretch'd his brain,
Till he who ne'er ask'd quarter cried for peace.
To Gloucester went he—rather say, his friends
Convey'd him there ; and there went with him too
The one idea, the thorn-point of his soul.

As may in modern times some classic fane,

Whence the divinity hath fled, lay down
Its stricken glories on the vulgar earth ;
Great blocks of matchless sculpture strewn around
Attest how Nature, leagued with Time, can wreck
The works which challenge life beyond her own ;
While men stare at them, idly wondering
At those sad relics of gigantic art,
Like thoughts of beauty so impress'd in stone
That the type perish'd with the architect.
So on from day to day and night to night
The politic chief, the warrior-monarch lay,
Dissolving into the similitude
Of common workers toppled down by death ;
A human ruin, trusting all its fame
To fleeting memory, or historic tale.

   Thus many a mortal yet endures to heap
A pyramid of gold, or gather fame,
Or rule his kind—to end in what ? To leave
To a posterity that heeds them not

His name and deeds upon a hireling stone
In monumental mediocrity.

Friends spoke the king with comfortable speech
Of his ancestral glories, and his own;
How his great sire to France and Germany
Had sent five royal daughters of his house.
How the same France and Norway and Bretagne
Were blest with kings which he himself had giv'n.
He answer'd not, as if he heard them not.
They told him too his name would never die.
Then querulously he : "But I myself?
I see Death coming like a conqueror
Who sacks the outmost town, and breaks the guards
That fence a nation's heart, until he knock
With rude hand at the very central core
From which the life-blood flows to all the land.
O ! that he were a bodily enemy
Whom I could grapple with in open fight,
Eye watching eye, and hand opposing hand !

This have I done—this shall I ne'er do more!"
And as he raised his hand, past memories gave
The nerves a short-lived firmness—then it sank
With the lean fingers drooping from the wrist.

    The abbot likewise, now with greyer hairs
And portlier presence, as the gift of time
And careful eating, took his proper turn
Of whisp'ring comfort, naming the good life
That they who do good here hereafter live.
He instanced the king's gifts to God's own church
As given to God—his costly charities—
The fetters knock'd from slaves ; then Athelstan
Cried low as from a sudden twist of pain ;
And men remark'd it, pitying him, and said
It was the fell disease that wrench'd him so.

    One too, a courtier—such as courtiers were
In those old days ; a man of subtle mind,
Who loved not fighting for the fighting's sake,

But who could fight if hard press'd, and the stake

Were worth the risk, yet rather loved to filch

The good thing by half-sanctioned trickery ;

But notwithstanding had the wit to 'scape

From being call'd a coward by his foes—

He, with the thought to please, told sneeringly

How Anlaf fled unwounded from the fight

Which the king won from him at Brunnaburgh ;

And settled down respectably, though young,

In some far quiet spot of Ireland—he

Could not for his part see how any nook

Of Ireland could be quiet—then the king

With strength unlook'd-for cried out testily,

"Go on !" and on he went, " Men say beside

That Bertha, when she heard how very sore

The battle went against him, join'd him there,

And there"—here Athelstan brake in on him

Wrath-reddened, " Not yet finished ! but go on !

What do they there ? Say on !" Then he (surprised

At being urged to speak, considering

He loved to speak, and spoke of what he loved),

"There do they live ambitionless and dull,

Kissing each other without change, as if

The world were nothing to these fools of love ;

She, doubtless, using all her charms to bring

The amorous heathen to the cross of Christ,

And he content to find his Heav'n in her.

I'd lay a cask of Gascon wine against

A horn of home-brew, that, to please her lord

She'll work his exploits in embroidery—

Especially his deeds at Brunnaburgh—

As curtain-hangings for their marriage-bed !"

But when the king had heard the glib account,

With painful force he raised himself and cried,

Half-shriekingly, " Begone, thou wretched fool !"

Then faint, sank back, while those around him said

He was too ill to understand a jest.

Nearer, and nearer came the conqueror,

Almighty Death, and shook the very door

That led into the inmost room of life.

But why describe a progress by all Time

Made common ?   Flowers or thorns which smooth the

    path

Or make it sharper leave the goal unchanged.

One day ; a day of rest, for pain had left

The body of the king, and e'en the mind

Had gain'd brief respite from the vulture fang

That tore it with unsatisfiable thought,

He sent for Edmund : Edmund hasting came,

When Athelstan with undetermined voice,

As timorous of the answer which he ask'd,

And, with a look which, if it ask'd not pity,

At least moved pity in the seer, said

" My brother ! speak the truth to one who soon

Will speak no more to thee or other man.

Have I done to thee as I should have done

In all the parts of life and in God's sight ?"

Prince Edmund knelt beside the sick king's couch

And cried in faltering tones, " Thou hast, thou hast—

Done all things I can think thou shouldst have
    done,

In all the parts of life, in sight of God."

Lighting the hollow face of Athelstan

A smile broke forth, as if one, suddenly,

Should place a candle in a skeleton's skull,

Then tired of jesting, put it out, so died

The smile to darkness, and that death's head grew

More ghastly than at first. The suffering Prince

Lay, motionless awhile, save a slight throb

O'er all his limbs from earnestness of thought ;

Then, in a questioning whisper cried, " Not so !

I cannot with the good I've done, o'er-lay

The evil that Heav'n's eye shall see it not.

Art thou right, Eadgitha ? O Christ !" and here

A gentle look of hope, not painless quite

Took up its dwelling on his face, and thence

It never past, not even when the arm

That levels kings had fall'n on Athelstan.

Then did he lay his hand on Edmund's head,*

That great hand which had stretch'd out once to reach

An empire, and had caught and held it fast—

Now weaker than a child's—and said, with voice

That seem'd to snatch at the retreating breath,

"Avoid to do as I have—brother, hear.

I do confess," but from the courts below

Suddenly burst a most untimely clash

Of horns and battle-trumpets, and such sounds

As warriors love when heart and arm are fresh,

Drowning his feeble words, and when they ceased,

---

* This prince, who succeeded Athelstan on the throne, was obviously less deserving of elevation than Edwin would have been. His life, like his brother's, was full of action, and his death more tragical. Many historical interests are invested with greater grandeur, but few excite a more thrilling interest. Seated in the midst of his nobles in the Gloucestershire village of Puckelchurch, he beheld an exile, whom he regarded with peculiar hatred, enter the banqueting hall, and take his place at the board. Forgetful of his dignity, the king rose from table and sought to expel the intruder by force. A hand-to-hand encounter took place. The combatants fell, and rolling together on the floor, the king at length obtained the upper hand, and lay on the prostrate body of his foe. Unable to extricate himself, Leofa, the exile, drew his dagger and plunged it into his antagonist's heart; after which, as might have been expected, he himself was cut to pieces by the armed and infuriated guests.

Edmund heard nothing save a murmuring moan
From lips that moved as struggling hopelessly
Beneath a weight that closed them ; and his hand
Slid gradually off from Edmund's head,
And falling hit the bed with a sharp sound,
As if its last blow were for ever struck.
Prince Edmund started to his feet, and turn'd
His look aside, in terror to behold
What he knew must be seen, then, timid glanced
Into the king's face, now no more a king's,
And saw beneath him, quench'd eternally,
The light of England, Athelstan the great.

The young Prince trembled thus to stand alone
Where erst had been himself and Athelstan,
The first of living men, but nothing now.
A wailing spirit seem'd to fill the room,
The voice of Glory mourning for her son ;
And Edmund look'd again, half doubtingly
Upon the prostrate form, as if once more

It *must* arise to rule the souls of men,

But not a motion stirr'd the couch of death,

And not a sound disturb'd that night of day.

    What follow'd ?   Scarcely after such a life

Had stopt its motion, is it worth to tell

How next there came the solemn vanities

That wait on great men's exits, vanities

That have their use when men are vain and weak—

The panoplied remembrances of death ;

And ostiaries and melancholy bells,

And exorcists that sprinkled holy dew

To damp the ardour of encroaching Hell ;

And acolytes that held their tapers high,

As crying unto all men, " Ye who think

Your deeds are evil, come not to the light !"

Then in long lines of men and warlike sounds,

The noisy show of military grief,

And martial trumps that once led on to war,

Now shriek'd lamenting as if war were dead.

The warriors of all ranks, as slow they march'd,

Held in their hands their helmets, fenced with skins

Of wild beasts, or, more costly, iron-gilt.

Behind their backs were bound their sounding shields,

As if all use for such things had expired

With the imperial soldier they bewail'd,

And as the train swept on to Malmesbury

Bearing the body of King Athelstan,

Rich gifts of gold and silver went before,

And saintly relics heralded the corse ;

And thick behind came troops of mourning men—

Monks whom the king had gifted splendidly

With miles of land ; and they whom he had fed,

Being indigent, from his benevolent farms.

The slaves whom he had freed, brought up the rear

Beating their breasts, and wishing Heav'n had spared

Yet longer for the earth so good a man.

And the old men, whom fruitful length of years

Taught all things, cried, " How great was Athelstan !

How wise in council, and how strong in fight !

And how he loved his country—how he wore

His life away in thinking good for her ! "

Then pray'd for sons that might resemble him.

And all the women cried, " How beautiful,

How full of princely grace was Athelstan ! "

They praised his smile, his eyes, his shape, his hair,

And wish'd their daughters husbands like to him !

And all the young men cried, if they could do

As he did, only for a single month,

That were enough of life for any man.

Wrapt in fine linen, with his battle-arms

('Mong these the dagger pledged at Beverley

Which he redeem'd what time he turn'd his steps

Victorious from the fight at Brunnaburgh)

In the grey-marble coffin by his side,

Beneath the altar-stone at Malmesbury,

In the great church, they left the king alone,

Unseeing all the honours paid to him,

Unhearing how the people talk'd, and said

What happiness it was to be so great.

THE END.

www.ingramcontent.com/pod-product-compliance
Lightning Source LLC
Chambersburg PA
CBHW020348030726
47496CB00007B/2053